CU00847724

# HIDDEN LIVES

Kestral Gaian

First Edition Printed 2017


ISBN: 1540707407
ISBN-13: 978-1540707406


www.KesGai.com

To Katharine, Skylar, Lucy,
and all my friends at Bosco Lounge.

## Prologue

"She's dead! She's not coming back, okay?"

It was dark and foggy. Dustin was sitting on a bench, unable to see more than three feet in front of him, as he used the last of his energy to yell at the slender figure in front of him.

"How can she be dead? What's happened to her, Dustin? Where's she gone? Seventeen year old girls don't just disappear without a trace. Her Instagram hasn't been updated since the start of the summer, she's stopped posting Snapchat stories, and the last person I know she spent any time with is you."

"Listen, dude. I loved her. I know she was messed

up, like you're messed up, like Alice, and Steven, and Aaron... but I loved her. I accepted her. And now all I've got left is a sodding hair band and a bunch of useless photos!"

As he spoke, he threw the bag containing the photographs and hairband toward the figure. Dustin looked up, but could barely see his assailant through all of the fog. If you'd just happened upon this scene, you'd never guess that it was the middle of the summer holidays—it looked more like the setting for a Christmas card.

"Who are these people? Steven... Aaron... your accomplices? How can you expect me to believe a word you say when you won't tell me where she is or what's happened to her, and then just start reeling off random names?"

The voice of Dustin's antagonist seemed oddly disembodied as a result of the thick white haze, making the anger and frustration in it seem somehow more threatening. Dustin began to sob, overwhelmed with the emotion of the situation.

"I can't tell you any of it. I can't tell *anyone*, okay? This is so damn hard for me."

"Hard for you? Someone's *dead*, Dustin, or at the very least missing. And right now I'm not convinced that you weren't the one to make it happen."

"Piss off." Dustin said, standing up and storming towards the fog-covered figure. "Get the hell out of my life."

He stormed forward and pushed the mysterious person to the ground. Shaking with rage and anger, with tears running down his face, he began to run through the fog until he found a familiar footpath. He stopped to catch his breath and, leaning against a tree, began to sob to himself once again. Pulling his phone out of his pocket, he realised with a start how late it was.

"Damn, I was meant to be home hours ago."

He unlocked his phone and flicked to the photos app. There, in his favourites, were several photos of him and Emma that he took a few weeks previously. Dropping his phone to the ground, he put his head in his hands and began weeping heavier, until eventually his whole body was shaking.

"I love you, Emma. What am I meant to do now?"

## Chapter One

Aaron awoke with a start. It was still dark, and a cool breeze washed over him from the open window next to his bed. He ran his hands through his hair— his forehead was clammy, and he noticed with annoyance that he had sweated through his bedsheets again.

He hated summer. Always had. Far too hot, far too humid, and never enough unbroken sleep. Bad dreams always seemed to find him in this weather, although come rain or shine they'd been increasing in frequency since the start of the year. They were often along a recurring theme, not that he could really remember much more than that once he'd woken up.

Looking over at the window, he found himself musing on the nature of dreams and reality, you know, the kind of heavy thoughts that one has at 3am. He remembered something his dad had told him at his twelfth birthday party, just three weeks before he was killed in an accident involving a drunk driver and an articulated lorry:

"Son, nothing makes you think as deeply or think you understand the universe as much as teenage hormones do. Trust me, you'll realise it's all crap soon enough."

It was one of the few things his dad had ever told him that he really resented, even in spite of all the health issues he'd had since his father's death. Surely not *all* of his thoughts and theories were the result of meaningless teenage bollocks? He turned his head toward the open window and looked out into the night.

The moon was full, and illuminated the land around the house. No front garden, no back garden, just land and trees. He could see ground fog in the distance, the result of hot weather interacting with one of the nearby lakes, but once his gaze broke the tops of the trees it was a beautifully clear night. On a night like this you could see the stars in all their glory, and even a bit of the Milky Way. He used to spend hours at this window as a younger child, looking up at the night sky and dreaming of traveling to distant worlds. This window inspired his love of physics, his love of science, and fuelled a life-long obsession with science fiction that so few of his friends shared.

Funny, he thought. The window was as much a metaphor as it was a reality. It had allowed him to see into his dreams and figure out what he wanted to do, what he wanted to be. Was this the kind of deep and meaningful rubbish that his dad was talking about?

Aaron sighed. This was no good, all he was doing was laying here stewing over whether he could trust his own thoughts or not. Annoyed and weary, he closed his eyes and laid back on the sodden pillow. Shifting his head around to find a spot that was a little less drenched, he quickly and quietly drifted back off to sleep.

\* \* \*

All around was fog. Eerie, glowing fog—like there was something just out of vision that was glowing, burning bright. He sat on some kind of bench, alone, and yet voices—people chattering—filled the air around him.

Every now and then he could make out the odd word or sentence—"Help me!", or "Where am I?" seemed to resound most often—but even if he stood up and spun right around, he couldn't work out which direction they were coming from or see anyone to whom the voices might belong.

He sat back down on the cold, hard bench and gazed up into the all-encompassing fog. Where was he? Was he dying? Or dead? He tried to steady his breathing and focus. He'd been here before. He recognised the place, in spite of there being no familiar features. He felt oddly at home here, in this dense formation of cloud.

Suddenly something flapped in front of his vision. Was that a bird? No, it couldn't have been. It didn't feel like a bird, there were no cries or feathers, no wings or claws. Aaron waited. Counted. Five, four, three, two, one… there! There it was again! Something dark, like a slight shadow in the fog, swooping around in front of him.

Aaron sunk further down on the bench, letting the fog envelop him. Another shadow. Two, three, four of them. Was it his imagination, or was their swooping getting more frequent, too? The voices seem to get louder as the shadows approached. "Help me," one cried. "Murderer!" yelled another. Where *was* he?

The bench on which he was sat felt solid. Hard, cold, but definitely intact—the only tangible thing in this place, it seemed. He ran his hands over it, feeling out from his shivering body. Smooth. Empty. Cold.

Another swoop. And another. The voices seemed to be getting louder and louder, and before Aaron knew it they had turned from muted statements into screaming cries for help. The shadows were swooping ever closer and more frequent and in spite of their lack of wings or physical form, they were whipping the air around Aaron into a frenzy. The fog seemed somehow more dense, the lights more intense, and the chill in the air altogether more biting.

Pressure started to build up in his skull. At first it felt like a run-of-the-mill headache, but with each passing second it seemed to grow ever more intense.

More swooping. More screaming. More pain.

The pressure in Aaron's head grew more intense, and it felt like his skull was trapped in a vice. Seconds passed slowly as the pain burned hotter, and the voices in his ear perforated his ear drums. Suddenly the intensity of it all reached a threshold and the floodgates opened. Aaron found himself involuntarily screaming out in agony, trying to release the pressure that was slowly destroying his cerebellum.

He wanted out of here. He wanted help. The pain was intense, like nothing he had experienced before in his life. It was all-consuming, overpowering, so much so that he even started pleading with the shadows: "I'm dying! This pain… help me! Save me!"

In the distance a new sound, like a truck reversing, started to cut through the screams. It grew louder, and Aaron finally couldn't take the pain any more. He curled up his fingers, grasping firmly at the edge of the bench on which he was sat, breathed in as hard as he could, and let out the most guttural, blood-curdling scream he knew how.

***

Sitting up suddenly in bed, still screaming with all of his might, Aaron opened his eyes. Gone were the shadows and fog, replaced instead by the familiar surroundings of his bedroom. The voices of despair and pain were suddenly replaced with birdsong flowing in through the open window, and the buzzing noise that seemed to split his skull came gently out of the alarm clock nestled between two books to his left.

"These dreams are going to kill me" he said aloud to no-one, as he swung his legs out of bed and surveyed the world around him. His brain was buzzing, but the softness of the carpet beneath his feet felt oddly reassuring. "It's okay, I'm safe, and I'm guessing Mum's already gone out or she'd have stormed in here wondering what the screaming was all about" he again exclaimed to the empty room in which he was sat.

Standing up unsteadily, Aaron lumbered over to the chair he'd thrown yesterday's clothes onto before he got into bed last night. At five foot eleven, he wasn't small for his age—nor was he a giant. He picked up the plain black t-shirt from the chair and threw it on over his still-wet forehead.

"Okay," he said, looking at his tired reflection in the mirror. "Let's see what today brings."

## Chapter Two

The ride into town was always a pain. No matter how many times Aaron cycled these tracks, it always seemed needlessly complicated and far too long a distance. He cursed under his breath at the fact that he lived so far away from civilisation as pushed down once again on the pedal of his worn out bicycle. Looking around him, he could appreciate the appeal of the natural beauty of the place—woodland and trees, shrubs, birds. It was rare to find a place like this in such a scummy town. But here he was, cycling through a veritable paradise in the hazy light of the late afternoon, on his way to the small grimy shopping district that

Meriville had to offer.

He thought back to the note that he hastily shoved into his pocket before leaving the house, keen to actually get to the shop after a lazy morning spent watching stuff on Netflix. "Kleine," it read, "Out at a committee meeting. Any chance you could pick up a few bits for us? Mama x" There was a list attached with a few items on it, from the mundane stuff like milk and bread to the frankly disturbing, like butternut squash. "What even is it?" Aaron asked himself as he cycled. "It's just orange mush. Weirdest. Vegetable. Ever."

He hated when his mother called him Kleine, and yet she insisted on doing so at every available opportunity. Who wants a pet name that translates as "little one"? It was embarrassing enough when he was five, and it was still embarrassing now some twelve years later. At least ninety per cent of the world around him had no idea what it actually meant thanks to their relevant ignorance of German language. The one advantage of having a foreign mother, he thought.

At seventeen years of age, Aaron Grayling stood tall and broad. While acne had not been kind in his younger years, his face these days was round and slim, with a vague hint of fluff about it. Forever grateful that he couldn't grow a beard, Aaron found himself too lazy to clear away the soft fuzz that inhabited the sides of his face particularly often, giving his features a soft, almost peach-like appearance.

In spite of the fact that he cycled everywhere he could, he seemed to completely lack muscle definition. His clothes just kind of hung off his gaunt, skinny frame to the point where he even looked upon the obese with vaguely jealous eyes. For Aaron, looking like a skeleton was very much for life, not just for Halloween.

He slowed his bike to a halt and stopped in the middle of the dirt track that led through the woodlands from his house to the town. The growing pains in his knees were there again, and he desperately needed to stretch a little before he carried on with the journey. Massaging his Lycra-clad knee, he surveyed the scene in front of him. The woods had always felt lonely and derelict. There were a few old huts and buildings here and there, mostly now reclaimed by nature after the railway line and station to which they used to belong had closed several decades earlier, but aside from those and the track that was heavily trodden into the ground, all he could see were trees.

He continued to rub his knee, which still felt like it wanted to break itself in half. He wished he'd stop growing already—one of the main reasons he had started wearing his cycling gear for every trip into town was because half his clothes were too tight to be comfortable whilst on his bike, and while it was fine in the summer, things would start getting cold soon and nobody wants to be freezing in a thin layer of Lycra.

Aaron remembered with a grimace the time he told his friend at school a few years ago how much he liked his cycling gear. "It feels amazing! Here, touch it" he remembered saying to David, his best friend at the time, who looked back at him bemused. "You're weird, who wanks over Lycra?" One Google search later, and Aaron knew he wasn't alone—but didn't dare tell any of his friends again.

"Right" he said out loud, as if to clear the bad memory from his head, "back to it."

As the path beneath his wheels turned from compacted earth to concrete, the trees started to thin and more signs of life were visible to Aaron as he sped along on his bicycle. The change from the vibrant green of summer leaves to the dull, raging grey of a town that was suffering from severe neglect was jarring to say the least.

Meriville wasn't a huge town, but it was far too big
to be a village and far too small to be a city. Nestled
in woodland just off the M6 motorway, its
population of around fifty thousand people tended
to be one of two things: unlucky, or criminal.
Sometimes, they were both. Aaron would say he'd
always been on the unlucky side of the spectrum.
With strong morals that he'd inherited from his dad,
he was the one who often spoke out against the
thieves and bullies in the town,… in his own, quiet
way.

Buildings loomed closer. Aaron was grateful to the
town council for finally, after years of campaigning,
building some secure bike storage in the town
centre. While vandals had tried their hardest with it,
the metal structure had managed to maintain
enough strength to stay together and still be a useful
thing to lock a bike up inside. Leaving his prized
cycle inside its steel innards, he got his hoodie out of
his bag and headed around the corner.

Ahead of him was Meriville town centre in all its
glory. While it had been here for several hundred
years, it had been rebuilt shortly after the war and
turned into a 'New Town'. Re-built in the 1960s, it
took the phrase 'concrete monstrosity' to entirely
new levels. The cracked, greying buildings that lined
the roads and rose up to three or four stories in

places blocked out most of the natural light, and ancient, barely-functioning street lamps hung precariously from cables strung up between the buildings. At some point, an architect sat down and saw this as a vision of the future. Now it just looked tired, and nothing like the old town with its Victorian railway station that he'd seen in pictures dotted around the old pubs and historical buildings in the area.

Walking past the pound shops, charity shops, and armed forces recruitment places, Aaron couldn't help but wonder what this town looked like in its heyday, before social entropy set in. It must have been bustling, a real beacon of hope and glory in the days when pomp and circumstance ruled the waves. Still, he wasn't planning on staying here forever. Why would he? Nothing good happened in Meriville—possibly the dullest town in the world.

Shaking himself to his senses, he walked toward the supermarket and grabbed a trolley. Pulling the note out from his pocket, he re-read the shopping list that his mother had left for him. "Just a few things" he muttered under his breath, "just a few backbreaking things and then I'll be home again."

## Chapter Three

There he was again. Dustin. Did he ever go home? Aaron knew that he went to the college in Trentham, but he always seemed to be here, in the poorest excuse for a supermarket ever, in dreary old Meriville. He always seemed to look impeccable, too. It often annoyed Aaron how great Dustin managed to make a standard issue Tesco uniform look, especially since the guy seemed to work here twenty-four hours a day.

"Hey, weirdo" Dustin called out as he noticed Aaron push his trolly haphazardly into the aisle he was working in. "How's life?"

Aaron smirked. At first, being called a weirdo by Dustin had started out aggressive, almost in a bullying way as the two interacted as kids. These days it was more affectionate, with Aaron coming to realise that Dustin was just as weird, in his own not-quite-so-obvious way.

"Dustbin," Aaron replied. "Still enjoying life as a shelf stacker I see?"

"Well, it pays the bills"

"What bills? You live at home, you've got a free bus pass, and you basically eat nothing."

"Fair point, Weirdo. But you don't know what I get up to after work" Dustin finished with a wink.

Aaron shook his head at Dustin and pushed on down the produce aisle, trying to hard to control the wobbly-wheeled deathtrap of a trolley he seemed to always end up getting. Why can supermarkets not create something a bit less… well, a bit less awful, let's be honest, to push your shopping around in? Aaron was forced to move and contort all over the shop to stop the metal menace in his control from knocking over old ladies and piles of well stacked products. As he turned into the dairy aisle, he noticed Dustin leaning against one of the refrigeration units looking at him quizzically.

"Cycle shorts and a hoodie" joked Dustin. "It's a bold look."

"Yeah, and I suppose a Tesco uniform is the height of fashion?"

"At least my fruit and veg department isn't on display for all the world to see."

"Did you actually want something, Dustbin? Or are you just here to insult me?"

"Dude" Dustin said, gently grabbing Aaron's shoulder. "I just wanted to make sure you were doing okay, that's all."

The pair were now face-to-face, alone in the cold dairy aisle of the supermarket. Aaron scanned Dustin's eyes for signs of laughter or joviality, but only found sincere, almost sad eyes looking back at him.

"Seriously, I'm fine. Are *you* okay? You're acting… well, you're acting. It's not like you to show human emotion."

"Hey, just because I don't show it, doesn't mean it isn't there. But come on, man. We've known each other for years."

"Yeah, and we've barely talked. Ever. You used to

harass me, now we just sort of… well, we exist. I know you, you know me, but we're not exactly close enough for a heart to heart."

"Okay, man." Dustin removed his hand from Aaron's shoulder and patted it a couple of times. "Let me know if you want to change that, okay? I'm here. I've not exactly got a ton of friends myself."

"Who needs friends?" Aaron muttered under his breath as Dustin walked down the aisle and around the corner, presumably to resume his shelf stacking duties. How confusing. Aaron wondered what Dustin had meant, why he felt like he needed to ask if he was doing alright. Perhaps something was up with him, and that was his way of reaching out for help? Aaron felt a twinge of guilt. Why had he tried to connect with him? And why was Aaron so keen to shoot him down? He stalked off to the frozen foods section to get the last few things on his Mum's shopping list, head deep in thought about what had just happened.

## Chapter Four

The journey home was always worse than the journey there. The hills were steeper, and it was later in the day so the sun just didn't penetrate the trees as much. The summery woodland turned into a danker, more humid beast later in the day, and Aaron hated cycling through it in reverse.

He started thinking back to his odd encounter in the supermarket. He barely saw Dustin, usually only when he went shopping or occasionally around and about the town. Why was he suddenly acting so friendly? And what was with the weird comment about his shorts, anyway? Not that he was complaining. It was nice for someone to notice, he supposed, but it was one of the last things he would have expected to hear from Dustin.

The main thing bugging Aaron, though, was Dustin's eyes. They almost had tears in them. They looked so sincere, and so full of emotion. Where was all of that coming from and—more confusingly —why was it aimed at *him*, someone he's barely had a full conversation with in months.

The path continued wind around the woodland, the only change to normal being that, about thirty meters ahead, a large chunk of stone lay in the path of his bike. Not that Aaron would notice, as he was still in his own world thinking about how people of his generation would probably never be able to afford to buy a house anyway.

Twenty meters. Ten. Five.

Aaron's bike wheel hit the rock, and he went tumbling over the handlebars. The Lycra he was so fond of ripped on the rock itself, and blood started oozing from several small cuts up his legs and arms. Usually at this point Aaron would swear loudly, but having face planted the floor, he just lay there, letting the pain wash over him.

Eventually, when the pain had subsided a little, he slowly started to roll over and achieve sitting position. The light was fading and he couldn't see clearly, but he didn't feel like anything was broken. His face felt intact if a little bruised, and he only had some minor cuts. The most annoying thing was his cycle gear. He'd need to replace the shorts completely.

Standing up and staggering over to his bag, he pulled out his phone and opened up the text conversation with his Mum. "Came off bike, probably need a bath when I get in. Home a bit late."

Aaron kicked at the stone that caused his accident. It didn't look huge, but it was definitely out of place in the middle of the cycle path. He took off his front bike light and scanned the area, seeing an old brick hut just a few feet in from the side of the track. It was covered in undergrowth, weeds, and vines, but a quick comparison showed that the rock in the path was in fact a lump of brick from this old building.

Throwing the brick into the hut, Aaron expected to hear the clack of stone on stone, but instead the sound was muffled, like he'd dropped it onto a piece of carpet. Tentatively, he shone his bike light into the hut to investigate, and on the ground covered in a few leaves, and the newly thrown piece of brick, was a moleskin notebook.

Aaron got closer. The notebook looked well worn, and the pages were curled up at the end from what he guessed was damp. It had obviously been here for quite some time. Looking over his shoulder, he placed one foot into the hut and reached in toward the notebook. It felt cold and dusty, and he could see that it was filled with writing.

"Should I…" he said aloud to the trees, hoping that somehow one of them would respond and tell him what he ought to do. "I mean…" he continued, trying to convince himself that it was okay to open the book and read the contents. "Well, I guess I ought to start at the beginning."

Aaron sat down on the cool ground next to his bike, the cuts on his legs now forgotten as the dried blood formed scabs that would surely irritate him later. Turning the first page, he found oddly neat handwriting spelling the words 'This is the journal of X.A.R.' "A journal?" he said aloud. "Maybe I shouldn't… well… just a little." He turned the page and began to read aloud:

"I can't trust my own mind, or my memory, so I'm writing all of this down as I investigate this one. There's been a murder in this town, and I'm determined to get to the bottom of it."

"A murder?" Aaron asked out loud, questioning the words he'd just read. "Is this real?" He flicked through the pages of the journal to see diagrams, sketches, and meticulous notes. A photo fell out from one of the pages that pictured a boy looking out over the sea. He couldn't have been older than nine or ten… this couldn't be the author, surely? Perhaps this was victim? Aaron flicked back to the first page and continued reading:

"The police are no help. They won't even talk to me any more, and keep threatening to arrest me for wasting their time. I need to take the investigation into my own hands and find out who killed Emma, before more people in Meriville fall victim."

Aaron froze. Meriville. Here, this town. Maybe this was more real than he first thought. There must have been fifty pages of notes here. Skipping ahead to the final few pages, Aaron suddenly spotted a familiar name. Dustin. He started reading aloud again:

"Talked to Dustin again today about this. He still doesn't believe me, but at least he usually listens. Today though he was acting stranger than I've ever seen him be before. He tried to comfort me, and I must confess I got quite angry with him. It's not my feelings that matter, I need to solve this case! Why won't anyone believe me? Everyone just sees me as the weird kid, just like they always have."

"Dustin? The same Dustin from Tesco?" Aaron sighed, cradling the book in his hands. So much was running through his head—is any of this for real? Who is Emma? And who the hell is X? Suddenly Aaron's eyes were drawn to the top of the page and he dropped the book in terror. "The date…" he stammered aloud. There on the page, right above the paragraph about Dustin, was a date. Yesterday's date.

Aaron jumped to his feet and started pacing. "How could this have been written so recently? The book looks ancient. Who writes a book and leaves it in an abandoned hut? And what the hell is going on with all of these people? A murder? None of this makes any sense." He stopped in front of where he'd dropped the book and stared down at it. "Dustin *was* acting really weird today. He sat back down and picked the book up again.

"Everyone just sees me as the weird kid" he read again. Dustin felt an overwhelming sense of empathy towards whoever this person was. He'd always been the 'weird kid' too, and he knew how that could make a person feel. Perhaps this was something to be taken seriously after all?

Aaron reached for his bag and pulled it toward himself. Fumbling around in the front pocket he managed to locate a pen and, pulling it free from the bag, he took off the lid and sat with it poised over the book.

"I must be mad," he said aloud, as he put the ball of the pen to the paper just below the last entry and wrote 'I'm Aaron. I think I believe you.'

## Chapter Five

"You're late!"

The deep, gravelly voice of Aaron's mother echoed around the house as Aaron pulled his bike into the dirty conservatory of the dilapidated building he called home. He really hadn't realised how late it had got—between his random encounter with Dustin and finding that journal, he'd somehow lost track of almost three hours.

"Sorry!" He said insincerely, his mind still very much occupied by the mysterious journal he'd found.

"Your text said you came off your bike? Is your

medication making you light headed again?" His mother's voice grew louder as she came down the stairs and into the kitchen. "Are you okay?"

"Fine, Mum." Aaron pulled the shopping bags from his bike bag and hauled them onto the kitchen worktop. Closing the conservatory door behind him, he turned around just as his mother entered the kitchen.

"Look at the state of you!"

Magda Grayling stood and surveyed Aaron through her thick-rimmed glasses. She was not a small woman—natively German, she very much fitted the stereotypically stern look that the media seemed so fond of portraying strong women from that part of Europe as. In her late 40s, she had hair so tightly coiled that it could power a watch for several millennia.

She sighed a heavy sigh looking at the sorry state of her son stood in the kitchen. He wasn't lying when he said he'd come off his bike—but he seemed entirely unaware of how terrible he looked. There were cuts and scratches all up his legs, some of them deep enough to scar if he wasn't careful. His shorts were ruined, not just because of the tears that now perforated the front of both legs but because of the blood that seemed to be spattered all over them that was now dried to the point of probably never coming out in the wash. His face was bruised, his hair covered in earth and dirt—this was clearly a worse fall than he seemed to realise.

"Is your bike at least okay?" she said, wanting to get the mundane things out of the way before she stopped to check that Aaron was feeling alright.

"Oh, yeah, the bike's fine. It's just my shorts that are ruined." he said with a sigh. He *loved* these shorts.

"Wer den Pfennig nicht ehrt, ist den Taler nicht wert" Magda said through gritted teeth as she started to unpack the shopping that Aaron had hauled onto the counter. "At least you didn't ruin any of the vegetables. How about you go clean yourself up before your scabs come open and you drip blood everywhere."

"Huh?"

"Aaron, look at yourself. Did you hit your head, or black out? These are some serious cuts and bruises."

"Oh, I guess I didn't feel them. No, I didn't pass out or anything."

"Well, go and get yourself cleaned up. The last thing you need is *more* health problems."

"Mum, I'm *fine.* Honestly."

"Alright. Well, go get yourself cleaned up and get an early night or something."

"Na gut. Gute nacht, Mama."

"Gute nacht, Kleine."

In spite of his hatred of the affectionate pet name his mother still insisted on using, Aaron managed to feign a smile as he left the kitchen and headed up the two flights of dark, carpeted stairs that led to his bedroom. The floorboards creaked as he lumbered his way up, his legs stinging as he started to realise the extent of his seemingly minor accident.

Aaron's bedroom was on the top floor of what seemed to be a lazily-built victorian farm house. The place definitely needed work—there was the odd patch of damp here and there, and the floors and walls seemed to creak if you so much as sneezed loudly while you were indoors. He loved the place, though, in spite of it feeling empty with just him and Magda living there.

Reaching the top of the stairs he pushed open the heavy wooden door to his room and reached around inside for the light switch. He'd always taken good care of his own space within the house. It was generally clean, and he'd been allowed to add a few extra plug sockets and a couple of decent light fittings to it over the years. This was his space, his castle. His home.

Aaron stood in front of the mirror and surveyed himself. His Mum was right, he looked *Unheimlich*. He moaned aloud as he touched his shorts and realised that they were completely wrecked, and then took a sharp intake of breath as he ran his fingers over the cuts on his legs. These were deeper than he thought they were, and now that he was home they damn well hurt. He walked over to the sink in the corner and wetted one of his purple flannels. "This is going to hurt in the morning" he said as he sat on the old stool he kept in the corner of the room and started to clean up his wounds.

For the first time since he got back on his bike and rode away, he let his thoughts turn to the journal. He still wasn't sure what made him write a response to that entry, but he knew that ink is indelible and that, short of going back and destroying the damned thing, he wasn't going to be able to undo it now. Had there really been a murder in Meriville? Why wasn't it on the news? He suddenly had a thought—maybe his Mum would know. He carefully stood up, ensuring he wasn't dripping from any of his newly-cleaned wounds, and opened his bedroom door a crack.

"Mum?" he called downstairs.

"Yes, Kleine?"

"Do you know anyone called Emma?"

There was a pause.

"Not any more, dear. Now goodnight."

"Wait, not any *more?*"

"Yes, well, it's a common name. Good*night,* Kleine, and don't forget your medication!"

"I won't. Night."

Aaron closed the door and sat back down on the stool. Not any *more?* What was *that* supposed to mean? He shucked his torn-up shorts, shrugged off his hoodie, and peeled off the rest of his cycle gear. At least the top wasn't damaged, he thought to himself. Standing in his underwear, he shook the dirt from his hair and once again stood in the mirror surveying his reflection and stretching to relieve his now aching muscles.

"So someone has been murdered, someone called X is investigating, Dustin is involved, and I've just left my name in X's journal like a muppet. Aaron, you're an idiot."

As he performed one final stretch, he sniffed his underarms and recoiled at the smell. "Jesus, I need a shower" he said as he looked his own reflection in the eye. "Tomorrow. First thing." He said as he walked over to the light and flicked it off. Darkness enveloped him and his bedroom, but he moved over toward his bed instinctively and laid down atop the duvet. Aaron sighed, reached over to the tablets on his bedside table, and popped open the lid. "I can't even remember what these ones are meant to do anymore" he said, as he threw the tablet into the back of his throat and swallowed hard. Closing his eyes, he could tell it was going to be another hot, humid night.

"Life just keeps getting weirder."

## Chapter Six

Aaron was aware that he was naked, and that it was cold. Bitingly cold. The fog was somehow thicker this time, but that did nothing to dull the blinding out-of-reach light that always seemed to shine. He knew this was a dream—he'd been here enough now to be able to work that out right from the start, and he hoped that by acknowledging the dream-state he was in, he'd be able to have a bit more control over his surroundings this time.

"I know this is a dream!" he called out into the fog.

"He knows this is a dream" came a reply, almost like an echo, but sounding like fifty people's voices had all been combined into one.

"I'm Aaron. Who are you?"

No response.

Aaron reached down and felt the bench that he was once again sat on. It was as smooth as the last time he was here. Solid, no cracks or gaps, no features. Tentatively he stood up and, on realising that the ground beneath his feet was still there, started walking slowly into the fog. Looking down, he realised that the cuts on his legs were gone. This was definitely a dream then, he thought.

Something was different about the dream this time, but he couldn't quite put his finger on what. Walking forward, he had no real idea how far he had moved from his starting location—everything looked the same, the fog was just as thick, and he was absolutely freezing. He stopped to massage his arms and legs in an attempt to warm himself up.

"He knows this is a dream." The voices said once again, this time unprompted.

The penny dropped in Aaron's head, and he realised what was different about the dream this time around. Silence. The pleading, screaming voices that usually filled the air were all mute, save for the time they spoke in unison to repeat his initial comment back to him. It was the clearest the voices had ever been, and certainly the first time they had said the same thing at the same time. There seemed to be so many of them, too. Young and old, high and low, and every conceivable gender seemed to be represented in the maelstrom of disembodied vocalisation that inhabited this place. Aaron shivered. Somehow the place seemed even more unsettling than it did before.

He started counting his steps, taking one a second to keep track of his pace and how long he'd been walking for. One hundred, one hundred and one, one hundred and two... His feet were starting to feel like ice. He looked down to survey them, but the fog was so thick he could barely see past his midriff. He pushed on, counting the seconds.

Four hundred and ninety-nine, five hundred, five hundred and one...

Aaron stopped and found himself scanning around the fog. He could have sworn he saw a break in the light somewhere up ahead, but at this point he was perfectly prepared to believe it was a mirage. The fog was, after all, so all-encompassing he could be anywhere. But no, he was certain that if he squinted, there was something just off centre up ahead. A small, darker patch in the fog. Should he investigate? Or call out? No, discretion was probably best here, he thought, and started padding gently towards the spot that he was convinced was becoming darker.

Sure enough, as he approached, the dark patch in the fog gained more clarity. It was person-shaped, and as Aaron quietly edged closer he started being able to make out legs, and arms, and the clear outline of a head. And a shirt. A Tesco shirt.

"Dustin?"

No response.

"Dustin, is that you?"

Aaron ran the rest of the way to the shadow and found himself face to face with Dustin. His eyes were closed, and he was stood perfectly still—but there was no mistaking the familiar features of the person he knew and vaguely tolerated. He reached out a hand and placed it on Dustin's shoulders. They were cold but solid, feeling more real than anything else in this place had before. Dustin appeared to be in a deep sleep, and even shaking his shoulder did nothing to alter his breathing, his facial expression, or his somehow calm-looking exterior.

"What are you doing here, then? Is it because I saw you today? Or because you were in the journal?"

"He knows about the journal" came the voices once again.

Dustin hadn't moved—it certainly wasn't him that had spoken, but the voices referencing the journal gave Aaron a deeply uneasy feeling, like a pit had opened up in his stomach. The dream and the journal. Were they somehow connected? No, they couldn't be. He'd been having this dream for years, and he only found the journal today. It must just be because the journal was on his mind.

"What do you know about the journal?" he shouted into the fog, his hand still on Dustin's shoulder.

Suddenly the air around him started moving, as if a breeze were coming in. It grew stronger, freezing his already cold arms and legs and making his fingers numb. The shadows were back, flying around him and whipping the fog into a frenzy with him and Dustin in the middle of it all.

"The journal" they all said, suddenly not in unison but back to their dissonant, disorganised ramblings. The whole that they had become was once again chaos, flying around Aaron and the still sleeping Dustin, repeating the same two words over and over and over.

"Who is X? What does all of this mean?"

No further response came from the disembodied voices aside from the continued yelling of "the journal" as the shadows cycled like birds. Aaron craned his neck around to try and get a glimpse of one of the shadows up close. They kept flying close to him, but they were fast—the second he saw one it was gone, never more than a vague blur of shadow in the bright, dense fog.

"Aaaah!"

Aaron cried out in terror as he suddenly felt a hand on his arm. He turned to face Dustin, whose hand had found the arm still clutching his shoulder. No longer the picture of peaceful sleep, his open eyes were now engaged directly with Aarons with a clarity that felt like it penetrated his soul.

A smile flicked across Dustin's mouth and suddenly, in a quiet, compassionate voice that filled every corner of Aaron's being, he whispered a single word.

"Emma."

Aaron drew in a sharp intake of breath and quickly closed and re-opened his eyes. He was looking up at his dark ceiling, in his dark bedroom, alone atop his sheets. He reached over to his bedside table and picked up his phone. Opening the notes app, he quickly typed "Dreamt about Dustin. He said one word. Emma."

As he put his phone down, his eyes were drawn once again the the pill bottle he'd taken his medication from earlier. "Jesus" he said to himself quietly, "that's the last of those I'm taking. I can't take many more dreams like that." Exhaustion took over, and his head once again hit the pillow as consciousness slowly abandoned him and let him slip finally into a restful, dreamless sleep.

## Chapter Seven

For the next few days, Aaron didn't feel much like leaving the house. His legs were still healing, the bruise on his face looked like he'd gone for three rounds with Tyson Fury. He could barely stand to look at *himself* in the mirror, let alone inflict his current appearance on the rest of the world.

Besides, if he went out he might run into Dustin. Since that dream the other night, he'd been feeling odd about seeing him again. He decided that a few days away from the world that included him, the journal, and the mysterious 'X' would be a good idea, and so had been spending his time sleeping, watching Netflix, and generally trying to 'chill'.

It wasn't working. He felt totally stressed out and more tired than he did earlier in the week. Was it a result of laying off his medication, because school was starting again soon, or both? Probably both, he guessed. It was going to be his final year at Meriville Academy, having stayed at the small school for sixth form rather than opting for the college in Trentham like Devin and so many others from his school seemed to. The school just felt more comfortable to him. More familiar and more traditional, offering some of what his Mum called the "old style A Levels" that she'd spent years telling him were probably worth more than these "new-fangled BTECS." He still had a few days, though, and having already done all the coursework he needed to do before term started, he promised himself he'd try to enjoy some time not doing very much. He wasn't very good at it.

The journal wasn't giving his brain much of a break. No matter how hard he tried to distract himself, he couldn't seem to shake that mouldy old moleskin from the back of his head. Had he put it back as he'd found it? Would the author have noticed his hastily scrawled message? And what the hell was Dustin doing talking to X anyway? He never seems to talk to anyone, well, not when he's around Aaron anyway.

Maybe he ought to go and check it out, see if the journal was still there? He didn't want anyone to see him like this, though… perhaps tonight, after it gets dark, he'd sneak out and cycle back to the hut and see what the score was. Perhaps.

"Do you want some lunch, little one?" Magda's booming voice came from downstairs.

"Mum, I'm four feet taller than you." Aaron called back in  vague annoyance.

"That doesn't answer the question!"

"Yeah… Thanks, I guess I should eat something. I'll be down in a few."

Aaron swung his legs out of bed and stood up. Feeling his face and grimacing slightly at the pain from the bruise on his cheek, he looked around the room for some clothes to throw on. Anything would do, really, he just wanted to go downstairs and get some lunch… but he knew that his mother would just comment on how lazy she thought he was being if he didn't at least make some kind of effort. "Oh whatever, this'll do" he muttered to himself as he threw on some black jeans and a black t-shirt. "I can handle looking emo for a couple of hours."

\* \* \*

Magda was worried. Aaron hadn't been this out of sorts since his medical troubles started a few years ago, and she felt like she had perhaps given him a bit too much freedom and independence to deal with it all. She had to remind herself that he was almost an adult—and already old enough to pretty much do what he wanted—a fact that she hated her own parents for not respecting. This was different, though. This was her son, and maybe after everything he'd been through he needed more protection than she'd given him. She shook her head. "Denk nicht nach, Magda. Du weißt, was du tust."

"What's that, Mum?" Aaron said, as he entered the room. He looked tired, like he hadn't been sleeping well—but she was sure he'd been home for the past couple of days, even the times she'd gone out she had believed he was in his bedroom.

"Nichts, Kleine. Nothing."

"So what's for lunch? I'm starving."

"You've been in your room for three days straight, I'm not surprised!"

"I have eaten, you know… just not exactly what you'd call full meals."

"If you're not going to eat well, you'll end up either fat, or dead. Or both."

"Well you're cheery today!"

"I worry for you, son. How are you feeling? Are you stressed about school starting again?"

"A bit, I guess…" Aaron sat down at the kitchen table and poured some juice into his glass from the jug in the middle. "I'm pretty well ahead on the work front, so I'm not really sure why I'm anxious. I'll be fine, maybe it's just because it's my final year."

"Maybe, maybe. Brot zeit?"

"Yeah, that's fine, thank you. Anything I can do to help?

"No, no, you just sit."

"Thanks!"

Magda busied herself with the bread and the salami, throwing in some onion too. He seemed better this morning, somehow more with it. She relaxed a little. Perhaps the worries she had in her mind were all for nothing. She added some paprika into the mix, and kept stirring. Now firmly in a

world of her own, she jumped a little when Aaron
started speaking again.

"Dad liked brot zeit, didn't he?"

"Yes, he did. We had it often when we first started
dating. He was visiting Munich a lot on work and
didn't have a lot of time to meet me, so we would
have lots of short dates at lunch time when he could
sneak away."

"I wish… oh never mind."

"No, Kleine, go on. What do you wish?"

"I just wish he was here sometimes, that's all."

"I know. But you've got me, and -"

"But it's not the same, mama." Aaron interrupted.
Magda stood in silence, unsure how to react to what
very much felt to her like an insult.

"I mean… I'm sorry, Mum. I didn't mean for it to
sound like that. Like, I know I had twelve years with
him and everything, but I'm almost an adult and he
didn't get to see any of that, and… I guess I wish I
had. I wish I could talk to him about the stuff you
won't talk to me about."

"You can talk to me about anything, Aaron."

"Alright then, who's Emma?"

The silence between them grew for a few seconds before Aaron resumed talking, his voice sounding angrier and altogether more menacing than it did a few moments ago.

"Exactly. You're keeping things from me. Do you have any idea how that feels? I have no idea why, or what for, but I just feel like dad would have been more honest with me."

"Kleine… I…"

"Just leave it, Mum. I don't want to talk about it any more."

Magda turned back to preparing lunch, painfully aware of how defeated her son's tone was as he had finished talking. He was right, of course. His father probably would have been more honest with him, but she was far too far down the rabbit hole for that now.

\* \* \*

Aaron ate the sandwich that Magda had made for him and felt infinitely better than he did before. She was right, a proper meal did him the world of good, even if he'd further been able to cement the idea in his head that she was keeping something from him. Chewing still felt a bit sore on his left side where the bruise was, but the sandwich was really good, and he was determined to savour it while he had the chance.

He thought ahead to tonight. A plan was forming in his head—he'd keep on the dark clothes and cycle down to the hut with a bright torch in his bag to pull out once he was sure the coast was clear. He'd check the journal, and then head straight back home again. He'd be gone less than half an hour.

"Thanks for the sandwich, Mama. That was amazing."

"Bitte, Kleine. Ich liebe dich Sohn."

"Love you too, Mum."

Aaron climbed the stairs and prepared for his evening excursion, hoping that his mother would be in bed and sleeping deeply by the time he was ready to leave.

## Chapter Eight

Cycling in the dark didn't usually bother him, but tonight Aaron was being cautious. Not just because the last time he was out was the cause of his current bruises and still-healing cuts, but because he was wearing all black and trying to be as undetectable as possible.

The last thing he wanted was to come across 'X' at the moment he discovered his defilement of his journal, or to bump into anyone that might ask him why he might be out in the early hours of the morning wearing all black without his bike lights on. Usually a very cautious cycler, this whole situation made him feel uneasy and something of a rule breaker… not his style at all.

Rounding the corners, past darkened trees and sleeping shrubs, he pushed forward with the journal on his mind. Would it still be there? Surely any sensible person would, on realising someone had discovered it and written in it, choose to hide it in a different location. Who hides a notebook in an abandoned old stone hut, anyway?

He thought back to lunch with his mother earlier that day. Was she really keeping things from him? It's possible, he supposed, that she just knew someone called Emma from the dim and distant past. But what if it was the same Emma that featured in the journal? Could he rat out his own Mum to try and solve this case?

Up ahead the hut loomed into his peripheral vision, and Aaron slowed to a stop. Placing his bike up against a tree a few feet away, he grabbed the torch from his bag and slowly stepped closer to the target. His heart was pounding, and he couldn't help but breathe heavily—he was suddenly aware that he was terrified. What the hell was he doing here?

He came upon the hut and peered slowly around the open doorway, and let out a long breath. It was empty, no sign of X or any other human beings in the area. Aaron held up the torch and pressed the button to turn it on. He was almost blinded by the light, having let his eyes get so used to the dark, but at least now he could see for certain that there really was nobody in the hut.

In the middle of the floor, though, looking as decrepit and dusty as it did a few days previously, was the journal. It had moved from where he'd put it, against the back wall, and was now facing away from the door very much in the centre of the room. His breathing became heavy again… X had obviously been back, and yet still chose to leave the journal here now that he knew it had been discovered.

Aaron moved further into the hut, picked up the journal, and sat down on the spot from which it had come. Turning the intensity of the torch down to that of a smaller reading light, he unfastened the elastic holding the outside of the journal in place and flipped it open.

"Here goes" he whispered under his breath, and flicked through the pages to where he'd left his message. There was something new written underneath, with yesterday's date next to it:

'Came to read through my notes, and found that my

journal had been discovered by a third party. I can only assume that he is reading this entry now, so I shall direct most of the rest of at him. Hello, Aaron.'

Aaron stopped, clenching up as he read his own name. There it was, written in X's impeccable hand. He was involved now, there was no escape. He continued to read.

'I would usually introduce myself, but there's no time for pleasantries. If you believe me, then you know that there is a murderer on the loose in Meriville, and that I've as yet been unable to find them or ascertain who they are. You have two choices—either help me to find the killer and bring them to justice, or walk away now and I'll hide my journal elsewhere.'

So there it was, Aaron thought. His get-out-of-jail-free card. He felt a sudden sense or relief that he could just get out of this without having to do anything, but something compelled him to keep reading.

'Take the journal with you and read what is inside. If you want to help, tell me everything you know on the next page and we can work together. I'll return for the journal in exactly three days. If you want no part in this, just leave the next page blank and you won't hear from me again. Time is short. Farewell.'

Aaron closed the journal with a slam and coughed as dust flew up from the pages into his face. His eyes stang, and he rested the journal on his knee to rub the grit and grime from them. "So, I'm meant to take you home?" he said to the journal quizzically. Clutching the journal by the spine, he stood up and brushed himself down with his free hand. "So much for being incognito" he mused aloud, as he noticed the effect that the dust had had on his black clothing.

He turned off the torch and left the hut. The air was a little cold, and he was feeling exhausted now that the adrenaline and fear was wearing off. Reaching the spot where he'd hidden his bike, he reached for the zip on his saddle bag and pulled it open. "You'll be safe in here" he said to the journal, treating it as if it were a living breathing thing. "At least until I get you home. Come on."

With a yawn, Aaron threw his left leg over his bike and pushed away from the tree. The cycle home was short, but he couldn't shake the feeling that the journal was like a lead weight in his bag, pulling him downward, dragging his entire being below the ground. What *had* he got himself in for?

## Chapter Nine

Sitting up in bed, Aaron sighed. His Mum had brought him up a cup of tea while he was sleeping, and he suddenly panicked that he might still look like he was covered in dust after his late night excursion—but a quick glance across the room at the mirror gave him a small bit of relief—he looked, for the most part, like his normal bed-haired self.

He grabbed the tea from his bedside table and took a sip of the steaming hot liquid. Magda had clearly left it for him just a few minutes ago. He picked up his phone—devoid of notifications as usual—and opened up a new text message: 'Thanks, Mama. Just what I needed :-)'

A reply came in quickly. 'NP, Kleine. Popping out, back in a couple of hours.'

Aaron stretched out and cradled his tea, sipping it soothingly as he curled up his toes and enjoyed the comfort of his bed. He felt oddly relieved and refreshed, comforting himself with the realisation that no matter what happened next, he wasn't about to get arrested or killed for snooping through someone else's diary.

He put his tea down and picked up the journal that he'd placed underneath the table on his return last night. Turning it over and over in his hands, he realised that he'd once owned a very similar looking notebook. Through the dust and dirt and dried leaf residue ingrained in the cover he could just about make out the initials X.A.R. scratched neatly into the leather.

He scanned around the room, feeling far too lazy to get out of bed, and reached for a nearby sock on the floor. It wasn't exactly clean, but he balled it up and began to work it across the covers and outer spine of the book in an attempt to clear away some of the layers of grime that inhabited it. Slowly but surely the layers of dirt gave way and the book regained some of its original black shine, even if only in places. There were scratches, as if the book had seen a lot of action, and the dirt just wouldn't come out in some of the more grime-filled areas.

He threw the now filthy sock across the room in the vague direction of his dirty laundry basket, and pulled at the elastic that held the book closed back cover to front. With the pages finally free, he gave the journal a shake. Several things slid out of pages, including the photograph that he found the first time he saw the book. Picking it up, he looked at it again with brief curiosity before putting it on the table beside his bed and turning his attention to the various clippings and pictures that had also fallen from the journal.

There were several newspaper cuttings from the past three years that covered a variety of local events, from the groundbreaking ceremony for the new local primary school and the rat infestation at Tesco through to the discovery of the ancient plague pit on the other side of the recreation ground. Various words and phrases had been highlighted and a few notes like 'investigate this further' were scrawled in the margins and over some of the photos, in which the odd face had been circled.

"I suppose I'd better start at the beginning, then" he said to the book, opening the now somewhat cleaner cover and flipping past the first couple of pages he'd already read. The date of the first entry was from just over six months ago, but the same impeccable handwriting looked up at him from the page.

'It would seem that Emma has been missing for six weeks. Dustin hasn't seen her since they had an argument after his shift one night and while he won't tell me what they argued about, he repeatedly tells me that it's not his fault that she's gone. I only knew her through him, but it is now obvious that she is missing and he is uninterested in investigating. I went to the police and filed a missing persons report, but Dustin wouldn't tell me her surname. They pulled him in for questioning, but released him half an hour later with no charge. Neither the police nor Dustin will tell me what they discussed, so I'm taking matters into my own hands. Current suspect: Dustin James Loom. It's too early to rule out police corruption and possible collaboration. The game is afoot.'

Aaron reached for his tea and took another sip. It read almost like fiction, but somehow involved someone he knew. X's meticulous attention to detail in recording his current prime suspect's full name removed all doubt from Aaron's mind—it was definitely the same Dustin. It seemed that he and X had a mutual friend, or at least acquaintance. The words in the journal gave Aaron the feeling that X knew Dustin far better than he did. He flipped over the page and read the next entry.

'Seven weeks now, and still no sign of Emma. Went back to the police today, and they threatened to charge me with wasting their time if I went back in again. Went to see Dustin earlier and showed him several old news clippings I found in the library archives to see if any of them were Emma. He refused to even look at them, and told me that Emma wasn't coming back. An interesting statement. Does this mean he knows more than he's letting on? My only suspect continues to be Dustin James Loom. More people must be involved, someone can't just disappear without a trace—and the police are an absolute joke. I intend to head back to the archives tomorrow.'

Below the entry was a sketch of Dustin wearing his Tesco uniform, with labels like "he must own five shirts" and "three pairs of these". Clearly whoever X is, he's obsessed with the idea that Dustin seems to have something to do with Emma's disappearance. Whoever Emma is. Aaron picked up his phone and wondered momentarily if he should try calling the police himself. Would they believe him any more than they'd have believed X?

He felt the sudden urge to talk to Dustin. He didn't have his number, but he'd probably be at Tesco as always, stacking the shelves or sitting behind one of the tills. But no… he thought he should perhaps just read a bit more, and decide if he actually wanted to get involved first. He turned the page.

'Eight weeks. This is now a murder investigation. I widened my field of enquiry and found more people who knew of an Emma, but none of them were willing to discuss it, or had just said they hadn't seen her in a while. The archives proved fruitless, and I have since been banned from taking more newspaper clippings from the library. Somehow I get the feeling that my investigation is being hampered deliberately. I am no longer as certain that Dustin is involved. I pressed him for more information again and he broke down, becoming very emotional. He said he knew she was gone, but that he couldn't explain how or why. He gave me a bag with some of her belongings in—a hairband, a guitar pick, some polaroids of them together, and a photograph of a boy by the ocean. I took the bag and its contents, but I plan on returning them should I see him. I feel that he needs them more than me, but have included a few details sketches below. Current suspect: unknown.'

Several pages of sketches followed that entry,

detailing the guitar pick, the hairband, and a few other things that were obviously related in some way, shape, or form. There was a blank page, too, which Aaron assumed belonged to the photograph that was currently sat on his bedside table.

Aaron had read enough, and felt like he had to get involved. The message from X had said to tell him everything that he knew, so he flipped ahead to the first blank page in the book and grabbed a pen from the floor by his bed.

'Okay, I'm in. I want to help. I don't know much, but I do know that Dustin was acting very odd when I saw him a few days ago. I don't know him that well, not as well as I think you do, but maybe I can talk to him and see if he knows anything? I don't know who Emma is, but I want to help you catch her killer. I don't feel safe knowing that there's a murderer on the loose, and the police clearly don't care. Let's work together. Should we meet to talk? One other thing…'

Wanting to write more, he flipped over the page— just as he heard the front door shut and his mother call out "Kleine? Ich bin zuhause, you okay up there?"

Hearing her footsteps on the stair, Aaron panicked,

quickly gathered all of the newspaper clippings and loose illustrations that were strewn over the bed into a pile and shut them inside the journal. Snapping the elastic back over the cover, he just managed to stow it under his pillow and lay back down in bed before Magna knocked twice and, not bothering to wait for a response, opened the door to his bedroom.

"Never heard of privacy, Mama?"

"Aaron, dear, ich habe das sagen. You might nearly be a man, but you're still my baby boy."

"I'm going to go red at this rate, Mum."

"It's a mother's job to be embarrassing. Anyway, are you doing fine?"

"Yeah, I've just been stretching out and drinking that tea."

"Shall I make you another, lazy boy, or are you getting up now?"

"Another one wouldn't hurt… thanks Mum."

"Okay, Kleine, I'll just take your cup and- "

Magda paused mid sentence and looked alarmingly at Aaron's bedside table. Momentarily confused, Aaron followed her gaze and his heart froze. He'd forgotten to put the photograph back in the journal, and his mother was now staring at it with a look that seemed half anger, and half shock. The silence in the room became tangible, almost painful, and Aaron searched for something—anything—to break it with. Much to his surprise, Magda beat him to it.

"Aaron" she said, her voice very slow and measured. "Where did you get this picture?"

"I—err—I was rummaging through a box of old stuff the other day and found it in there. I just got it out to take a look at it again this morning."

He was never particularly good at lying, but on this occasion his mother seemed to believe him. She reached down, hands trembling, and picked up the photo from the bedside table. She looked at it with the same confusing expression for a few seconds, before seeming to snap herself out of it and putting the photograph in her back pocket.

"Let the past be the past, little one. I'll go make you some fresh tea."

She picked up the empty cup from Aaron's bedside table and began to make her way out of the room, leaving Aaron confused and alarmed by what had just happened. The past? The photograph? What the hell was going on.

"Mama!" he shouted, just as she was about to close the door. It was almost a reflex action, and it took him a few seconds to gather his thoughts and think of what to say next.

"The boy in the photo... who is it, anyway?"

A long pause followed. While Aaron couldn't see Magda, the was still stood just the other side of his bedroom door, hand on the doorhandles, frozen in place. After what seemed like an eternity she responded, voice slightly breaking as she did so.

"That, dear... is your father."

The handle turned and Magda closed the bedroom door behind her. As her footsteps grew quieter, Aaron was left alone, sitting upright again in his bed, unable to move or think or breathe under the weight of the words that his mother had just spoken.

## Chapter Ten

Meriville Academy was not a new school, nor was it a well funded school. Like most of the early academies, it had been granted a few pots of cash here and there when it changed its name from the somewhat plainer 'Meriville Secondary School' a few years ago, but none of it had been managed particularly well, and the only real changes were a few new signs and some unnecessarily complicated recycling bins.

From outside the school gates, you'd be forgiven for thinking this was a really posh school. They were old wrought iron, with a large 'M' on one side and a large "S" on the other. Vines crept up the old brick pillars that held the gates in place, almost giving the place the appearance of a stately home fit for an Agatha Christie novel. This illusion sadly stopped once you stepped through the gates.

Cracked tarmac led from opulence to obvious neglect, as the path gave way to a makeshift carpark and the small block that housed reception, the head-teacher's office, and various other parent-facing facilities. Nestled behind that, and sprawling out in an manner that looked very much like a drunken octopus trying to tap dance, were the remainder of the school's buildings and grounds. The tallest, at four stories, housed maths, science, computing, and —bizarrely—music. It was also the most 'normal' looking out of all of them, resembling a grey, dreary office building circa 1970. Just in front of the grey monolith that the students jokingly called 'death block', separated by an uneven brick-lined walkway, was the somewhat less imposing languages block. This building looked like a plump person squatting in sand—it was painted pink and yellow, with curved wood lining the outer walls in what looked like an architect's attempt to 'funk it up a bit'. Behind that, the humanities block stood at a modest three stories, but with twice the number of windows and far less concrete it looked far happier than Death Block did. Last but not least was the hall, sports hall, drama studio, and newer 'multi purpose rooms' that only ever seemed to get used on parents evenings. It was the newest building there, but looked like it had just been thrown onto the land like a die, and they left it where it landed. If rumours were to be believed, it was meant to be central and a bit more square-on, but the guy reading the building plans was going blind and didn't tell anyone.

George Croft stood outside main reception and surveyed his kingdom. Not much had changed over the summer, other than the fumigators coming in to get rid of the bug problems they had in the languages block and the removal of the bees nest that had appeared directly above his office window. He always found the place eerie yet peaceful before the start of a new term—empty, but somehow ready for the energy that 2,400 youngsters were about to unleash on the place.

He took his phone out of his pocket and turned up the music he was listening to. Ironic, he thought, that in just five days he'd be telling students off for having their headphones in. A thought struck him, and he unlocked his phone, opened up the music app, and switched the track to Rebel Rebel by David Bowie. George didn't need anyone to tell him he was the coolest head-teacher in the world, he thought to himself. Moments like this just proved it.

He walked through the sliding glass doors of the reception building and made a beeline for his office. Taking his phone from his pocket and pulling out the headphones, he placed it into the speaker dock he had on the small coffee table he used for informal meetings, set the music playing again, and made his way over to the high-backed, leather swivel chair that sat behind his desk.

For the first time in years, George felt ready for the start of the new school year. This *never* normally happened, and he had spent the best part of the last three hours checking and double-checking every to-do list he had to ensure he hadn't forgotten anything that might blow up in his face come September fifth. If there was then he couldn't find it, and nor could either of the deputies that he'd emphatically delegated to over the past few days.

On his desk, completely covering his laptop, desk phone, and any stationery he'd left laying around, were the few remaining posters that he hadn't found a suitable space to put up around the school. This year he'd designed his own motivational posters, rather than going with the insipid rubbish that the local authority sent over. He knew 'cool' better than those office-dwelling freaks.

A knocking noise pulled George out of his own head and back to reality. "Come in" he called out in an overly-cheery voice as he rummaged around the mess on his desk to find the remote control for his stereo. "No students here yet, no need to stand on ceremony!" He found the remote and turned down the volume.

"George?" came a small voice from behind the door. "Have you got a sec?"

"Always! Come in, come in."

The door opened and a short, young-looking man entered. Standing no taller than five foot five and looking like he could be a student, he timidly closed the door behind him and approached the desk that George was sat eagerly behind.

"Take a seat, Dan! How's physics going, all ready for the new term over there in death block?"

"We…. We try to discourage people calling it that."

"It's what the kids call it though, isn't it? No harm in a friendly nickname!"

"I… okay."

"So what can I do for you Dan? Don't look so scared, you know my door is always open to the teaching staff, especially our bright young NQTs! Are you excited to start your second year here?"

"Yes, thanks George, I am."

"Please, call me Crofty."

"I… I'd rather… just use George if that's okay?"

"Suit yourself. So, what *can* I do for you?"

"There's a new poster outside my room, and I'm not sure it's giving quite the right message to the students. I was wondering if I could take it down."

"Which poster?"

"It's the one that says 'Don't diss-lexics'. It's almost like it's making fun of dyslexia, with the whole misspelling. I'm amazed that the local authority would send these out, really, but I remember you saying last year that you weren't a fan of the fact that these posters were forced on us, so I was hoping you wouldn't mind if I just… removed it?"

"Daniel, Daniel… I think you're missing the subtle humour! Are you implying our students won't be able to tell the difference between a burn and a fleek?"

"I… you… what?"

"You see, it's funny *because* it's misspelling it. This poster is a riot!"

"Or it'll start one."

"Nonsense! The poster stays. It's part of a new set of inspirational and motivational literature we've been working on."

"So it's made by the same people who did the 'Pepe the Frog loves when you get good grades' and 'Harambe wants you to succeed' posters?"

"It certainly is. Whatever marketing genius thought those up ought to receive a bonus!"

"Err… okay. So the poster…?"

"The poster stays, Dan."

"Okay. Thanks George."

"Crofty!"

"Err."

"Anything else I can do for you?"

"Oh! Yeah, err, I've got a tutor group this year for the first time…"

"So you do! Year thirteen, the easiest year in the

school if you ignore the whole UCAS thing, which most of our students seem to."

"I noticed Aaron Grayling on my register. I'd heard rumours from Sam…"

"Come now, Dan! Don't believe everything you hear! Aaron's studious, competent, and a valued member of the school community. You'll love him."

"Okay, thanks George."

"Good luck, tiger!"

Dan timidly left the office and closed the door behind him, once again leaving George alone. George reached for the remote and turned the music back up, the song having shifted several times during his encounter with the young physics teacher. He sighed and looked at the posters strewn over his desk. One teacher's opinion didn't matter, he reassured himself. These posters were for the kids, and they'd get it. Come Tuesday next week, they'd all be queuing up to high-five the Croft-meister.

## Chapter Eleven

Aaron took his usual position in front of his full-length bedroom mirror and surveyed himself as he so often did. He'd grown a bit over the summer, as the pains in his knees were so fond of reminding him, and while he'd got new school trousers and new shirts, his blazer was now very slightly too small for him. He did up the buttons and tensed so that the fabric strained and made him look ridiculous. He should probably remember to ask his Mum to get him a new one at some point.

The uniform for Meriville wasn't the worst he'd ever seen. The standard combination of black shoes, black trousers, white shirt, and blazer was fairly typical. The bit he hated, though, was the tie. Keen to keep the 'school colours' alive, the board of governors had approved a new tie design a few years ago that could easily be mistaken for modern art. Stripes of lime, mustard yellow, and pink struck parallel with one another in a sort of criss-cross pattern up the tie's length, and there was a red weave that went up the sides that all-in-all made it look more like wrapping paper than a garment.

Still, here he was. First day of the new school year, his last year of sixth form, and the countdown to his final exams, final deadlines, and uni applications lay in front of him. Still in two minds as to whether to apply for physics courses, or combine it with maths or something else, the process of finding and applying to universities was the thing coming in the next few months that he was looking forward to the least. He'd put a lot of work into making sure his CV looked good and that he could pack his personal statement full of things that universities would love—but he was feeling uneasy about the changes that would come from leaving his small, comfortable life in the wonky farmhouse in the tiny town that he called home.

"Are you heading off then, Kleine?" came his mother's voice from down the stairs. "You wanted me to remind you how much you wanted to get to the school early today."

"Yeah, I'm almost ready. Just getting my bag sorted."

Aaron picked up his school bag and checked inside one last time. He had his folder, his textbooks for the day, his planner, and a few pens. That's all he needed, right? He checked and double checked his mental to-do list, and referred again to the timetable on the back of his planner.

"Yep" he said aloud to his reflection. "I'm ready."

Closing the conservatory door and pulling his bike to his side, Aaron was surprised by how warm September had started out being. Temperatures were almost as high as they were in the middle of the summer, and he knew that by the time he got to school he'd be sweating under his blazer. He wished he was able to wear his cycling gear for the rides to and from Meriville Academy, but with nowhere to change or shower when he got there, it was far easier to just ride to school in his uniform and hope against hope that there weren't any mud puddles on the way.

He hated lying to his mother, but he had no intention of getting to school early. Instead, he planned to stop off and check on the journal that he'd placed back in the hut two-and-a-half days earlier. It had been playing on his mind more and more, but with preparation for the new term at school he'd just not had the time to sneak out of the house unnoticed and check it again before now. Besides, he thought to himself, X might not even have had a chance to read it yet.

As he began cycling, his thoughts turned to the mysterious author of the journal that had come into his life. Other than what he'd read of their investigation, Aaron had no idea who or what X was, from simple things like gender or age through to where they lived, or what they did with their time outside of this covert murder investigation. He usually took pride in getting to get the measure of someone quite quickly, but X had him stumped, and that made him uncomfortable.

The warm autumn air whipped through Aaron's hair as he cycled through the woodlands that separated his house from the town proper. He loved this time of year—the nights were finally starting to get cooler, but the days were still fairly warm and dry. He could ride around without having to worry about waterproofs, and the woods weren't muddy or icy. Leaves hadn't really started to fall from the trees yet, but Aaron looked forward to the crunch of them underfoot before the cold weather came.

"My father" he said aloud as he stopped pedalling and let momentum carry him forward for a few meters. "She said that the photo was of my father."

His confusion over the photograph that he'd found in the journal hadn't abated in the days since his mother's revelation. It had been a long five years since his father's death, and he hadn't been able to pick out his father as a child in a photo He'd just assumed it was a random child. But no, apparently that was his father, and he'd forgotten his looks so much that he couldn't even pick his face from a crowd.

"But what was that photo even *doing* in that journal?" he asked no-one.

More than the shock of not being able to recognise his father from a photograph was the impossible reality that, somehow, his father was involved in this murder investigation. He'd been dead for five years —how could he have had anything to do with Emma? And why did she have a photograph of him in with her belongings?

A thought suddenly struck Aaron like a lightning bolt, and he slammed on his brakes. Stood straddling his bike, he tried to assemble the words now swirling around his brain into something coherent.

"Did my dad really die in an accident? Or was he murdered by the same person that killed Emma?"

He stood still, letting the weight of the words he'd just spoken sink in and penetrate his skin. It sounded ridiculous, almost something out of a fantasy novel, and yet there was a feeling in the pit of Aaron's stomach that told him his dad was involved, that this needed investigating. That it wasn't as far-fetched as it seemed.

Aaron got back on his bike and cycled slowly onwards, deep in thought about his father and the mysterious X. He'd be at the hut in a few minutes, and was starting to feel anxious about what he might find there. He'd ended up leaving a fairly long response when he got the chance to finish it, but had decided to leave a few details out—notably his mother's response to hearing the name Emma, and his father being the person in the photograph. He had to protect his family, after all.

'Lets meet to talk?' his entry had continued. 'Here's what I know. I see Dustin every now and then at Tesco. I wouldn't say we're friends but we know each other, and he was acting odd. Very odd, like someone had just died. He followed me around the store and at one point put his hand on my shoulder and looked me in the eye. His eyes were so sad. This was very out of character for him to be with me. I go back to school next week. Is there anyone there I should be talking to? I want to help. How can we solve this?'

Aaron had hastily thrown the journal back into the hut just a few hours after finishing his message to X, and he had felt apprehensive about it ever since. Was he throwing Dustin under the bus by talking about how oddly he'd behaved? And by not mentioning the revelations from his Mother was he doing nothing more than hampering or misdirecting the investigation? He saw the hut up ahead and slowed his bike down a little more. It looked like he wouldn't have to wait long to find out if his concerns were valid.

Leaning his bike against the old brick wall at the front of the hut, he stepped inside and took out his phone. Enabling the flashlight he scanned around the small interior. It definitely looked like X had been here, as the place seemed somehow tidier and oddly lived-in. Having caught some of the morning sun, the hut was a little humid and smelled like musty leaves and earth, like a well-used garden shed might. Looking around, the journal wasn't immediately obvious, but on kicking at a neat pile of leaves in the right-hand corner of the room he felt a familiar thud and there, beneath the rotting foliage, was the journal he'd come to know and revere.

He reached down and picked the journal up from the dirty ground. He'd made a mess of the hut by kicking the leaves out of the way, so he stood and leant against the wall to save getting his uniform dirty. Removing the elastic and flipping to the last page that had writing on, he could see right away that X had replied.

'No meets. It's not safe. We should investigate this independent of each other and share our findings here. Thank you for agreeing to help me. Now that I am not alone, we may make some progress. The weeks have continued to go by, and there is still no sign of Emma. I share your observation that Dustin has been acting oddly. I know him about as well as you do, it seems. I'd be interested to hear what his reaction is if you mention Emma to him directly. It would be so much easier to convince the police if there was a body or a clearer motive, but I've yet to find either. I've been exploring these woods, as well as the buildings and alleyways of Meriville. Nothing. I hope that we are able to find this killer soon before he, or she, strikes again. Aaron, see if you can get more out of Dustin than I could. And ask around at school to see if anyone else knew Emma. She must have had more friends than Dustin and James. Until next time, good luck.'

Aaron pulled a pen from his inner blazer pocket and, beneath X's entry, wrote 'I will update you soon. Aaron.' He re-fastened the elastic around the journal and placed it back on the ground. "Dustin and James?" he said aloud. "I don't know who James is, that's weird. I can always pop into the shop after school and see if Dustin is working." Getting back on his bike, Aaron thought ahead to school. He started pedalling at a faster pace, keen to get a space in the bike rack and make it to registration on time.

Today, he thought to himself, was going to be a long day.

## Chapter Twelve

"Good morning, everyone! No, no, that's not it. Hello! Too happy. What's up, my homies? No. Just no. Good morning, class. Yes, that's more like it. A bit of formality."

Dan Varley stood in his empty classroom, in front of the whiteboard on which he was projecting the words 'Welcome to 13DV'. He'd been at the school since seven that morning, pacing nervously around to ensure that every chair was in place, every desk properly aligned, and that his computer was working properly. He'd changed the font of the presentation he was projecting tens of times already that day, and had since moved on to practising his initial greeting to himself before the first students arrived.

The classroom was surprisingly warm for a physics lab. Dan had spent weeks over the summer perfecting wall displays and getting things ready for the start of term, with models of the solar system hanging from the ceiling and a display on magnets that had LEDs and was powered by a Raspberry Pi. This was a teaching room to be proud of, Dan thought, and he really did take pride in how interactive it all was. Usually he designed his displays with younger students in mind, but he'd been careful over the summer to try and include more for the older students this year, too.

He was more anxious than he had been taking his first lessons. Year thirteen was a big deal to him. They were the closest student to his own age, which made maintaining respect and boundaries harder, but it was also *the* year. Time to chose universities, decide on a future, start on the paths to who or what they wanted to be.

It didn't help that, with his diminutive size, all of the students at that age would tower over him. He'd always been short for his age, and was dismayed when he just stopped growing once he'd turned fourteen. Having tried and failed to grow a beard, and having spent time experimenting with tall-soled shoes, he'd come to accept his fate as a perpetually short person and turned his attention to the subject matter he knew and loved: physics.

He'd loved training to teach and found working with the younger secondary ages really quite rewarding. The older ones, however, just reminded him of bad times from his own school days. Agreeing to take on a sixth form tutor group was his way of trying to get over that. This was his Everest, and he was going to climb the hell out of it. He peered out of the window. Students were starting to file through the gates into the school. This was it.

* * *

"Good morning, class!"

Silence.

"Uh.. Welcome to 13DV! I know it's a bit weird having a new tutor group just for your final year at school, but when Ms. Fossey retired at the end of last year they had to put you somewhere, and so now you're stuck with me for a year."

More silence.

"Just… just a joke. Anyway, we'll go through the register in a minute, but I just wanted to say a few things first." Dan clicked the mouse on his desk and the slide on the whiteboard moved forward. "I'm Mr. Varley, and I teach physics. I went to university in Edinburgh, but I'm actually from Nottingham. I love the countryside, so much better for stargazing, and that's how I ended up living in Trenton."

He clicked the slideshow forward again, and the word 'respect' filled the screen.

"I… err… I believe in respect. And I don't mean that you should respect me, what I mean is that we should respect each other. It's my job this year to have your back, to help you get to where you want to be, and to make sure we do everything we can as a school to make you happy and fulfilled. How does that sound to everyone?"

Murmurs filled the room, however, none of them were of any discernible words.

"Okay, so, err, on with the register then. Atkins? Berg? Bolton?" he listed off the names of the 20 students in his tutor group, punctuated by "here" or "yep" from the students. "Ferguson? Glass? Ah, err, uh. Grayling?"

"Here" said Aaron, painfully aware of the odd pause before his name. Some of his classmates turned to look at him.

"Good good. Hass? Hayden? Knapp?.." Dan continued, finishing with "Stout? Webber? Great, you're all here. Well, registration today is short and sweet as there's an all-school welcome assembly, so you can all make your way to the hall now and I'll see you again at the end of the day."

Chairs scraped as twenty teenagers got up from their chairs and chatted amongst themselves as they started to file out of the room. Dan breathed a sign of relief at the fact that he'd made it relatively unscathed through his first interaction with the sixth-formers. He'd done it. He closed his eyes and rubbed his eyelids under his glasses. Opening his eyes again slowly, he jumped a little as he realised a student was stood right in front of his desk. It was *him*. Aaron Grayling.

"Sir," said Aaron "just wanted to let you know that I want to be a physicist, too."

"Y, you, err, you do?"

"Yeah, I love physics. I'm really happy that we get a physics teacher as a tutor, I'd love to get some advice from you about universities. Could I come back at break to talk about it a bit more?

"I, err, I'm pretty busy today, first day of term and all… maybe later in the week?"

"Sure, thanks sir. Seeya."

"Bye!"

Dan's heart was beating. In spite of himself, and the promises he'd made not to let gossip or rumour affect the way he treated any student, he had to admit that he was a little scared of interacting with Aaron Grayling. He shook his head, trying to remember the head-teacher's words. He seemed perfectly fine. But spend time alone with him? He sighed. At least he had year seven classes for the rest of the day. That should be easy.

## Chapter Thirteen

The first few weeks of the new school year dragged on boringly for Aaron, with his usual pattern of lessons and reading punctuated by all-school assemblies, fire drills, anti-bullying seminars, and various other activities that only served to distract and annoy students who just wanted to keep their heads down like he usually did.

More than the disruption to his routine that was taking away time from his all-important final year of study, He was feeling uneasy and distracted by thoughts of the journal, the murder investigation, and the hut in the woods. He'd exchanged a couple more communications with X, but hadn't been able to talk to Dustin since school started, and hadn't really stumbled upon any new leads, either.

It's not like he hadn't been trying to find out more, either. He'd been harassing his mother for more information on the picture of his father that had been in Emma's possession, but she outright refused to talk about it or let him see the photograph again. She'd even started avoiding him the more he asked, as if she were afraid that she might let something slip.

Aaron had been trying to see Dustin, too, but the two or three times he'd gone into the shop to find him he hadn't been working—a fact that, in itself, was worth investigating. He'd tried to go in a couple more times, but was starting to get funny looks from the security guard at the front of the shop since he'd been going in, wandering around, and then not buying anything.

He was starting to feel like he was being deliberately avoided and lied to, and it wasn't doing much for his mood. He sighed and looked down at the book in front of him. *Einstein's Universe* by Nigel Calder. It wasn't one of the course texts for A Level Physics, but he found Einstein's theories compelling, and really underpinned why he wanted to study it. He turned to page sixty-four and started reading.

"The shifting stars" he said out loud, reading the chapter title to the empty library around him. Nobody else seemed to bother with this place at lunch time anymore, which suited him just fine. "Redshift happens when light or other electromagnetic radiation from an object is increased in wavelength, or shifted to the red end of the spectrum."

When stuff moves fast it doesn't look the same, Aaron thought. Based on the dates in the journal, it had been twenty weeks since Emma's disappearance, but things weren't moving quickly then. Perhaps, he thought, if he could go back to the start and retrace her final days, things might shift out of the red end of the spectrum and back into visible light. They might finally be able to see clearly what happened to her in her final days.

He'd actually got used to thinking in terms of "they" now, too. He barely knew X, who still didn't want to meet face-to-face, but he felt like they were a team, investigating Emma's murder together, trying to piece together a puzzle that neither locals nor the police seemed to care about. They were heroes.

Aaron felt his phone buzz in his pocket, and pulled it out with little enthusiasm. A few days ago he'd set up a search alert so that whenever someone used the words 'Emma' and 'Meriville' in the same paragraph, he'd get notified. So far he'd learned that there's a six-month-old child called Emma in the town whose mother posts constant news about on Facebook, and that two local individuals think Emmental is spelled Emmatal, but had gained no further insights into the murder investigation or Emma's whereabouts. This time, though, he almost dropped his phone as he read the notification on his screen:

'New Instagram post by @DustyDustin: "Missing Emma :'-(" location Meriville URL https:// www.insta….'

He swiped the notification and unlocked his phone. The link sprang open on his screen and, after a few seconds of loading, the full update from @DustyDustin appeared. It was a black and white photo of two hands together forming a heart. One of the hands must belong to Dustin and the other, Aaron realised, must be Emma's. He scrolled through Dustin's Instagram feed and noticed the same picture posted further down, some twenty-six weeks previous. It wasn't a new photo. His heart sank a little—it wasn't a sudden miracle. She wasn't suddenly fine and with Dustin again.

But it *was* an update from Dustin, and the location tag was Meriville. Did that mean he was here in town, now? He checked the time. Still thirty-five minutes left of lunch break, would that leave him enough time to get to the shop, see Dustin, and head back again in time for afternoon lessons? Snapping closed the book in front of him and throwing it into his bag, Aaron got up and pulled his hoodie on over his black school blazer. He stormed towards the door with purpose in his stride and threw it open, making a clattering noise that—had anyone actually been in the library with him— would have surely caused upset. "Okay, Dustin…" he said aloud. "I've got you now."

\* \* \*

"Are you actually going to buy anything this time?" the stern-looking security guard said in a half-menacing, half-exasperated tone as the doors slid open and Aaron walked through them into the small, weathered-looking supermarket.

"It's lunchtime" he snapped back. "I'm here to get some lunch."

Aaron made his way to the produce aisle to see if Dustin was in his usual place, but couldn't see him there. He stalked up and down the various aisles of food and drink and homewares, his blood still pumping, his mind fixated on finding Dustin. Aaron was angry, something he'd noticed happening more and more since he secretly stopped taking his medication. This could be his chance, he thought. He might finally be able to catch up with Dustin and find out what he knows.

As he turned the corner, almost out of aisles to storm down, he walked straight into something solid. Dressed in a dark blue shirt, black trousers, and wearing a hat that belonged in a cheesy 90s cop movie, it was the security guard that he'd barked a reply at when he walked into the store.

"Uhhh… sorry." Aaron was feeling hot behind his ears—he'd been storming around in such a rage he hadn't stopped to think how that might look on the security cameras.

"Listen" the guard said, "I've seen you wandering around here for the past few weeks. I don't think you're going to take anything, or you'd have tried it before now, but you have *got* to either buy something, or get the hell out of here. Just what are you looking for, anyway?"

"My friend… he…"

"Oh, the kid that works here that's about your age? He's on the tills today, didn't you see when you came in?"

Aaron turned around to set off for the front of the store, but the security guard placed a firm hand on his shoulder and stopped him in his tracks.

"*Not* without buying anything, you got that kid? Go grab a sandwich or something."

The guard let go of Aaron's shoulder and walked off leaving Aaron stood alone, breathing heavily, trying to process the mix of adrenaline and fear that the encounter had generated for him. Dustin was here, and if he's working on the checkouts he'd be a captive audience. He'd have to listen, he couldn't run away. Aaron walked down to the aisle with all the savoury snacks and lunch things, picked up a hoisin duck wrap and a pork and apple pie, and made his way to the checkouts.

\* \* \*

Dustin was tired. He hadn't slept well recently, and he'd been trying to pull as many hours at work as possible to boost up his savings a bit now that he was in his final year of college. By doing so, of course, he'd been missing the odd lecture and not really focussing on coursework, but hey. He'd be able to make it up later in the year, he thought to himself, as he continued to scan through the shopping of one of the residents of the local old folks home.

He didn't mind working the checkouts—it was a lot less physical than his usual shelf-stacking role, but it was one he only really got to do when someone from the front of store team was off sick or something. He'd picked up Maria's shift today as she was off with the flu or whatever, and while it meant he was on until the shop closed at ten, it was a good chunk of extra, unexpected cash. And a distraction, too.

"Do you have a clubcard?" he asked the lady in front of him, her back bent and her hands shaking.

"Yes, dear, one moment."

"Lovely" he said, taking the card from the lady and scanning it with a 'beep'. "That'll be forty-four points and seven…"

"And what dear"

Dustin had trailed off as, while he was reading out the total to the elderly customer in front of him, he noticed that Aaron was now queuing at his checkout. Their eyes met quickly, just for a second, and Dustin was floored by what he thought was hate and anger flash across his face.

"Err, sorry. Forty-four pounds seventy three."

Dustin helped the old woman load her bags into the trolley and asked her hopefully whether she needed any help back to her car with the bags

"That's kind, dear, but I'll be fine. I like to keep active." And with that she was gone, leaving Dustin with no excuse but to serve Aaron. He sheepishly turned back to his checkout and looked at the conveyor belt.With only three items, Aaron could clearly have gone to a self-checkout, giving Dustin the idea that he was here specifically to talk to him. Looking up from behind the curtains of shaggy hair that covered his eyes, Dustin faced Aaron and attempted to smile.

"Hey weirdo!" he said in a faux-jovial tone. "How's it going?"

Aaron was breathing heavily, his eyes boring into

Dustin like hot needles.

"You weren't here."

"Yeah, even students get a few holiday days. I took some time off."

"*You* took time off? You never take time off."

"Well, this time I did."

"Why?"

"Dude," Dustin said defensively, starting to feel uncomfortable at how intense Aaron was being. "I'm allowed to take some time out if I want to. I just went away for a few days, borrowed my dad's car, toured around a bit. You know."

"Who with?" Aaron's interrogation technique wasn't subtle.

"I was on my own, Aaron. Just me and the car."

"Did you kill Emma?"

Suddenly, Dustin could feel the blood rushing to his cheeks. Tears burned behind his eyes, and the room around him started to sway with the confusion and rawness of what he'd just heard. He placed a hand on the counter in front of him to steady himself, and he forced his vocal chords—which felt like they'd locked themselves shut—to respond to his will.

"You…" he managed to rasp through the tears that were making their way down his cheeks from his now-red eyes. "You know about Emma?"

Dustin fell back into the tall chair that was waiting dutifully behind him. Usually he preferred to stand, leaving the chairs for the slightly older till workers who liked to sit down a bit more, but his legs had felt like they were about to give out on him.

"It doesn't matter what or who I know!" Aaron barked at Dustin, anger seeming to flow from every pore on his face. "What matters is what *you* know! Where is she? Is she alive? Did you kill her? Where's her body?"

Dustin began sobbing.

"Aaron, no. It wasn't… I mean… she isn't… She's just gone. Don't make me relive it, man."

Aaron stopped his interrogation and stood at the checkout, mouth open, looking surprised and almost regretful of the state that Dustin was now in. Dustin was clearly deeply affected by even hearing Emma's name, but he didn't seem fearful or guilty. He genuinely seemed sad.

"I… I'm sorry" Aaron said, looking away, suddenly

unable to face him. "I… I'll see you."

Aaron walked off, leaving his lunch unscanned on the conveyor belt. Dustin lifted up his head and watched Aaron as he walked down toward the entrance, through the double doors, and then he was gone. He caught his reflection in the screen of his till and realised that his eyes were red from tears. He lifted the little phone beside the checkout and dialled the numbers 4, 1, 3.

"Checkouts" came the curt voice at the other end of the phone.

"It's… it's Dustin on till fourteen. I'm not feeling great, could I take five minutes please?"

"You don't need to go home, do you? I'm already short."

"No… just need five minutes. While it's quiet. Is that okay?"

"Take ten, be back down here at 2, okay?"

"Thanks, Ann."

Dustin put down the phone, tapped the sign-out button on his till, and turned around to leave the checkout. "Oh, the stuff" he murmured to himself, realising that Aaron had left his lunch on the conveyor belt. He scooped up the wrap and the pork pie, and headed off to put them back on their respective shelves on his way to the break room.

## Chapter Fourteen

Aaron sat cross-legged on the floor of the hut, scribbling in the journal that he was resting on his knees, his bike light on the ground next to him providing just enough illumination for him to write with. Now that the nights had started getting shorter, he'd found it a little spookier and *infinitely* colder in the hut than it had been when he'd first discovered the place in the summer.

'I think I've blown it with Dustin' Aaron wrote, thinking back to his earlier encounter in the supermarket.

'I was angry, I saw that he was back in town on

Instagram, and stormed straight down there. I should have put a plan in place, or thought more about what I was going to say, but I just lost it at him. He looked…'

Aaron looked up from the book and put the pen down for a moment. How *did* Dustin look? He froze and stammered on hearing Emma's name, but then when he accused him of her murder he just kind of *crumpled.* Aaron felt a twinge of guilt as he looked back to the encounter, realising how much better he could have handled the situation. Picking up the pen, he wrote the only word that he felt could adequately describe it:

'devastated.'

'You don't react like that when you've killed someone. At least, I don't think you would. Dustin has always been a bit soppy, but his reaction today was just so full of emotion and longing… I don't see how he could have killed someone he clearly cared that much about.'

'It feels like we're getting nowhere, X. I think I need to try a different approach with people, see if I can do a bit of spying rather than being so head-on about it. How are you getting on? I'll try my new approach and get back to you in a few days. Aaron.'

He closed the journal, wrapped the elastic around it, and shoved it under the usual pile of dry leaves in the corner of the hut. It was freezing. Pulling his hoodie closed and throwing the hood over his head, he grabbed his bike light from the floor and made his way out of the hut and back to his bike.

For the rest of the ride home, his encounter with Dustin weighed heavily on his mind. He didn't quite know what to do about it—should he go back and apologise? Or just leave him? Maybe X would have a chance to speak to him… either way, Dustin now knew that he knows about Emma, so any semblance of cover was well and truly blown.

He got home and locked the conservatory door behind him. Taking off his muddy shoes and heading into the kitchen, he opened the top cupboard and stretched up to get a pint glass from the top shelf. Holding it under the tap, he filled it with cold water and took a deep drink. He hated hurting people. Before he could spend much more time dwelling, he heard the familiar creaking of his Mum moving around upstairs.

"Is that you, little one?"

"Ja, Mama."

"Have you had a good day? No, wait, tell me about

it when I come down, I'll just be a minute."

Aaron spotted a pair of his track pants on the radiator and felt them to see if they were dry. Vaguely satisfied with them not being entirely damp, he pulled off his school trousers and pulled the trackies on over his thin legs. Noticing that his school trousers were really dusty and grey at the back from where he'd been sitting in the hut, he threw them into the large washing basket in the corner of the room just in time before his mother entered the room.

"So, Kleine, wie war dein Tag?

"Oh, the usual. Just school."

"Or at least, just school in the morning?"

"How di…"

"The school always calls if you miss afternoon registration" his mother said, interrupting him. "Though they did call again to say you'd made it back halfway through the period after lunch."

"Yeah. I, err, I just went into town for lunch today rather than putting up with the stuff they serve in the canteen. I fancied something different, that's all."

"You're in year thirteen, your final year of study. You should be taking it more seriously."

"Mum, I know the course material so well already, the lessons are just boring!"

"Ja, ja, weil Jugendliche immer Recht haben."

"There's no point trying to defend myself, is there? It's fine, I only missed half an hour."

"Don't make a habit of it." She said firmly, ending the discussion. "Now, dinner in 10 minutes, okay? Go change if you want to.

"Okay, Mama. I'll be back down in a few."

Aaron left the kitchen and started to climb the stairs to his bedroom. "Oh, and Mama?" he called out, stopping and craning his head back down over the banister.

"Yes, Kleine?"

"Weil Jugendliche *nie* falsch sind."

\* \* \*

Magda watched Aaron as he ate, noticing how

quickly he was eating and how hungry he seemed to be. Where was he at lunchtime that made him 30 minutes late back to school? She was tempted to go down and ask at the shop, see if he'd been there— but no. That wouldn't be very trusting of her, and she needed to give him the space to do the things he wanted and needed right now.

"So how is this new tutor of yours? All I know about him is that he makes *me* feel tall."

"Ha, yeah" Aaron replied, genuinely amused. "He's an okay little guy."

"I hope you don't talk to him like that! What was his name again, Mr. Varnish?"

"Varley. And no, I haven't really spoken to him much to be honest."

"Oh, I thought that with him being a physics teacher and you wanting to go study it, you'd have loads to talk about! Didn't he do a physics degree too?"

"Yeah, he did, but I dunno." He sighed. "I've tried to talk to him a few times, even asked him directly if he'd sit down with me and talk me through uni options and stuff, but he just keeps making excuses and says he's too busy to do it. It's kinda annoying."

Like, hi, you've actually got a student here who's interested in your subject. He doesn't seem to care."

"Hmm, that's not very happy. I don't like the sound of him."

"He's okay, really, just not as good about the physics stuff as I'd hoped."

"I shall have words with that Mr Croft."

"I think he prefers to be called Crofty"

"He'll be called a great deal many things if I get my hands on him, Kleine."

Aaron laughed, and continued to eat his dinner with a smile on his face. Magda sat back in her chair, chuckling to herself. She enjoyed these exchanges with her son, he'd really inherited her sense of sarcasm and wit.

"It's good to see you smiling."

She got up from the table and picked up her already-empty plate. Walking over to the kitchen counter she placed it down next to the sink and sighed at the now teetering pile of plates and cups on the side.

"Will you sort out the dishwasher when you're done eating? I've got some things to get done upstairs."

"Sure thing, Mum."

Opening the fridge, she picked up the carton of orange juice that perennially lived in the compartment in the door, and shook it to see how much was left in there.

"Oh, and we need some more orange juice. Think you can stop by Tesco on your way home tomorrow?"

\* \* \*

Aaron lay in bed, looking up at the ceiling, his room vaguely illuminated by a combination of the charging LED on his laptop and the alarm clock that sat on his bedside table. It gave the ceiling, and the few other bits of furniture it cast light over, a dingy green tint like it was all just a reflection in a murky pond. He'd been trying to sleep for an hour now, but it just wasn't coming. Dustin was on his mind.

All his life, he'd been proud of being one of those people who didn't cause harm to others. And yet earlier, he basically attacked someone who'd shown him nothing but kindness in his own sarcastic way.

He was *angry*. And worst of all, he enjoyed doing it. He'd stood there with his heart pounding and his breathing heavy, like a hungry wolf, wanting to get information out of Dustin any way that he could. It was only after he reacted with such utter upset and visible trauma that Aaron had snapped out of it, left the shop, and taken a long walk back to school to shake it off.

Maybe he ought to start on his medication again, he thought to himself. If not being on it was making him angry, then it wasn't really going to help him. But those dreams… he didn't want to have another one.

"I guess I should just try it tonight, and see what happens."

He popped open the pill bottle and swallowed the first tablet he'd taken in almost two weeks. Setting his head back onto the pillow, he still felt wide awake.

Aaron moved his hand between his legs and found a familiar comfortable spot. Maybe that'd help him sleep, he thought to himself. He closed his eyes and let his mind wander.

Dustin and Emma were an item. That much was clear. X and Dustin are friends. Did X know Emma well? Who else knew her? Did his Mum have anything to do with it after her vague admission that she *used* to know someone called Emma? Images swirled around in his head, in spite of not knowing what any of these people really looked like. Well, except for Dustin. He looked tired today, almost like he'd barely been able to bring himself to shower or comb his hair or anything. Aaron wondered if he'd be there tomorrow when he went in to buy juice.

He was, at least, beginning to feel sleepy. Sleep was descending on him like a fog, and in his final moments of consciousness before it took him he had a sudden moment of clarity. His dreams—the fog in his dreams—he knew he'd seen Dustin in there because he'd made a note of it on his phone, but suddenly he was remembering more. It wasn't just Dustin that was in there.

He tried hard to remember if there were other faces, but all he could remember were black shapes, like shadows. There were definitely voices, though, He recognised some of them. Straining hard in his head to remember their intonation, he suddenly heard their voices again as if they were there in the room with him.

"Hey Siri" he called out to his phone. "Take a note"

"What would you like the note to say" the phone replied.

"The voices in the fog. They knew I was there. They knew it was a dream, they knew about the diary, and… and I think they might be in danger, too."

"Okay, Aaron. I've made a note." The phone replied, as Aaron's head rolled to one side. Tiredness had won, and he drifted into a deep, dreamless sleep.

## Chapter Fifteen

At this time of year, Dan's classroom was always cold first thing in the morning. Citing cost savings, the heating didn't come on until 8am, forty-five minutes before students started appearing at the school gates, but long after most of the teachers got to the school to start their prep for the day.

The rest of the physics department didn't have it quite as bad, but Dan had got the corner classroom with the two largest walls facing the elements. At this time of year, he could see his breath in the air when he first opened the door and turned on the lights.

This morning was one of those extra-cold ones, and Dan felt a shiver run up his spine as he sat down at his desk and booted up his PC. People would soon be talking about Christmas, and he vaguely wondered if he should put up decorations in his classroom while he waited for the computer to show him the logon screen.

By all accounts, it had been a relatively successful term. He'd been getting good feedback from his lower school classes, and his GCSE groups seemed to be thriving. Even his tutor group had warmed to him, with most of them saying that he "actually wasn't as bad as we thought you'd be". That was a compliment he was eager to accept, even if it was a little underhanded.

He began tapping away at his computer, finishing off his notes from yesterday's lessons and getting ahead of his plans for the day. He thought ahead to the extended tutor session he had this morning, and realised with a slight shiver that he'd have to spend even more time avoiding Aaron and his constant physics questions.

Okay, he thought to himself, maybe the shiver was from the cold and not from the student, but he still wasn't looking forward to it. He'd been trying for most of the term to get him to sit down and talk about uni choices with him one-to-one, and while he was keen to give advice to the group as a whole he just didn't feel comfortable sitting down alone with him.

The rising sun broke over the tall hedges outside the windows, and the room suddenly glowed a brilliant orange. Dan looked up at the clock—08:30 already —students would soon be arriving and he'd have a room full of sixth formers worrying about their relationships or their hair or their futures.

\* \* \*

"Alright everyone, it's PHSE day, so let's get down to the business of the day shall we?" Dan Varney stood in front of his class attempting to sound vaguely in charge of the rambunctious group of twenty seventeen and eighteen year olds that sat before him.

"We've got more to cover on the UCAS front today for those of you who are taking the university route, and some great new resources for those of you who are looking at apprenticeships or applying directly for job a bigger companies. The links on the board have everything you need, so grab yourselves a computer and get on it. I'll come round and see you all to make sure you're getting on."

The students moved to the computers at the sides of the room and started the long and drawn-out process of logging in and getting to a web browser. Dan took a sip from the now-cold tea that he'd made himself just before the students started to arrive, surveying the group in front of him. Nineteen of them, so one was currently missing. No surprises as to who, he thought. Connor Lucas had only been on time twice so far this term.

After a few minutes of taking the register and wishing he could go and make himself another cup of tea Dan started milling around the class, surveying their screens and offering pointers as to the mock UCAS applications that a few of them were filling out. He couldn't help but be biased toward those students planning to go to university, of which there were sadly only six. As a graduate himself, he was vehemently convinced that everyone should strive for a university education.

"Collins," he said to one of the students. He still insisted on calling them by their surnames. "The odd joke in a personal statement is okay, but do you think they really need to know how much you love your girlfriend?"

"It shows my commitment and dedication, sir."

"I don't think it shows your commitment and dedication to the *right things,* though Collins."

He continued around the class, pointing out the odd spelling mistake on work application forms and giving more vaguely helpful comments on people's personal statements. Then he got to Aaron's computer.

"Grayling, you appear to be Googling rather than doing your mock statement. What're you looking at?"

"University reviews, sir. Just trying to work out where I really want to apply to. I'd tried to talk to you about it a few times, but…"

"Ah, err, yes" Dan interrupted. "I haven't been able to find the time yet, with, err, you know, all the marking and…"

"It's okay, sir." Aaron pressed back firmly. "I get it, you don't want to talk to me about it. It's cool, I've found enough stuff online I think."

Dan Varney walked back around the room and sat down at his desk. He wondered whether Aaron had just handed him a blessing or a curse—on the one hand, he thought, he'd been handed a get-out-of-jail-free card. On the other, he felt vaguely guilty that Aaron had seemed to realise that he'd been making excuses. He had to keep reminding himself that these students were almost adults, not the same year sevens he was used to teaching.

Grabbing the cup from his desk, Dan stood up and straitened his jacket. Feeling confident that his students were all vaguely doing what they were meant to be, he stepped out of the room and slipped into the physics faculty office across the corridor.

"Hi Dan!" came a cheery Scottish voice from across the room, making him jump. He'd expected the room to be empty. "Escaping your sixth formers I see?"

"Just popped in to make another tea. Wasn't expecting to see you in here, Janet. All okay?"

"Aye, all good, just getting some stuff together before the day begins in earnest."

"Where's your tutor group, then?" he said, as he put a tea bag in his cup and flicked the switch on the kettle.

"Year nine are all out on the Wales trip this week. I've had four whole days without the wee little buggers. Utter bliss, Danny boy. Utter bliss."

"They're not that bad, are they?"

"What was it that my mentor used to say about year nines? They've got the maturity of year sevens, and the hormones of year thirteens."

"Ouch, that sounds tough."

"Not as tough as your day, I suppose?"

'How do you mean?" Dan tried to hide the concern in his voice.

"Our infinitely cool lord and master, Crofty, was looking for you earlier. He hasn't caught up with you yet?"

"Oh. No, I haven't seen him today. Did he say what he wanted?"

"Nope, just said he was looking for you. Unusual for him to come down to this neck of the woods, so I figured it was important. Anyway, I thought you might be in here escaping Mad Hatter Grayling."

"You mean Aaron Grayling? Why would I…"

"You've heard the rumours, right? Apparently in

year ten he spent twenty minutes screaming at his tutor. Word has it he completely lost it after his pa died, went full on mental, proper personality disorders and all that.

"He seems… quiet."

"Aye, well, it's always the quiet ones the say."

The kettle clicked off, and Dan poured the boiling water over the teabag. Giving it a stir, he scooped it out, threw it into the bin, and reached into the fridge underneath the kettle for some milk.

"Anyway, I'm sure whatever George wants it can't be that important, can it? I mean, he'd have tried harder to find me if it was, given me a call or something."

He poured in the milk and gave it a stir.

"I dunno, laddie. He always likes to give bad news in person."

\* \* \*

"Alright, 13DV, you've got five minutes left until the bell. Save where you're up to, and remember to click 'submit to tutor' so that I can take a look over them and give you some suggestions before next week. If you don't click it, I can't see it. And if I can't see it, I can't really offer you any suggestions."

The class around him convulsed with activity as students started to busy themselves with saving work, shutting down, and sorting their bags out for the rest of the day. Dan was a little anxious about what Janet had told him in the physics office, but kept reassuming himself that, had it been urgent, he'd have made an effort to find him and talk to him by now. He also couldn't shake the feeling that she'd been unduly unfair on Aaron. Surely teachers weren't supposed to talk like that, were they? He hoped that he'd never become that jaded and prejudice… even if he'd been pretty awful in his treatment of Aaron to date.

"Any last minute questions, anyone?"

Nobody responded, with everyone instead gathering around their desks and chatting away as if the last few minutes of the session were break time. Dan sat down, feeling reasonably satisfied that his selection for this particular tutor group would turn out to have been a fairly easy assignment to take on this year. His second year as a full-time teacher was turning out well.

The bell rang, and the class filed out, ready to head to their first real lesson of the day. Dan continued to sit at his desk, watching as his tutor group ambled from the room, sipping his still-warm tea. He had a non-teaching period next, and so he'd get to relax a little with some paperwork before the next class of the day arrived at his door.

A knocking sound wrenched Dan from his thoughts and almost made him spill tea from the cup he was still holding all over himself. "Come in!" he called from his desk as he put down the tea and smoothed over his jacket.

"Hi Dan, just me! Got a sec?"

It was the head teacher, Mr. Croft.

"George, sure, come in."

"I don't know if Janet mentioned, I tried to find you earlier on but then I thought hey, leave it until after registration. How're you doing?"

"I'm… I'm fine, thanks. The GCSE groups are doing amazingly well given the change in curriculum this year, and I…"

"How about your sixth formers" George said, cutting Dan off. "How is 13DV doing?"

"Uhh… Fine?"

"Fine."

"Yeah, I mean, they're on target with PHSE, no major incidents other than Lucas always being late, and…"

"So there's no reason we'd have received a phone call from a parent to complain about your skills as a form tutor?"

"I… what?"

Dan felt his cheeks flush. Someone had complained about him? But he'd been doing everything right! Why on earth would someone have taken the time to call in and make a complaint? Was he pushing them too hard to attend university? Or had he overlooked someone who he should have encouraged harder?

"Afraid so, Dan." George surveyed him for a moment, and then began to pace around the room as he continued on. "We've had a call from a Mrs. Magda Grayling. According to *her*, a certain student in your tutor group has been trying for weeks to sit down with you and chat about physics degrees. Apparently, or so Magda was telling me, he rather got the impression that you were avoiding him."

The head-teacher pulled a chair across the room and sat down next to Dan.

"Listen, Dan. You wouldn't be the first person to get like this, but it ends here, okay? Aaron is an exceptionally gifted physics student, and you'd do well to help him find a decent place at a university that will cater to his needs."

"I... err..."

"It's not open for discussion or debate. We don't discriminate on the grounds of physical *or* mental health here. I don't want to have another call from Aaron's mother saying that you're ignoring, avoiding, or otherwise not engaging with him, okay?"

"Yes, George. I'm... sorry."

"Don't be sorry, Dan my man. Just don't do it."

George Croft got up and walked toward the door.

"Oh and Dan? It *really* wouldn't hurt if you called me Crofty."

## Chapter Sixteen

The clip on Aaron's bike bag slid open, and he pulled up the top cover firmly. Possibly the greatest upgrade he'd treated his bike to, this bag was fixed permanently to the saddle and back mudflap, providing huge amounts of storage space for his school stuff, or shopping, or whatever he needed to carry around. It had the added advantage of doubling as an extra reflector, too, for the odd times he was cycling on the road.

He slid in the orange juice that he'd just bought for his mother—two cartons on one side of the bag, two on the other, and sighed. Dustin hadn't been there. He'd left school early so that he could catch

Dustin before the post-school rush of year 7s buying sweets, but with his trip to Tesco only resulting in orange juice, he was now running so early he could feasibly head back into school for the remainder of the last period.

He didn't actually have a lesson, though, so all he'd be doing is going back, doing not very much, and then coming home again, so he didn't really see much point. Instead, he could stop off and check on the diary, and get home nice and early for once. Hopefully his Mum would be out, or about to go out, and he could have a little privacy too.

Fastening his bike bag back up tightly, he slid one of his legs over the frame and lowered himself down onto the gel-padded saddle. He was disappointed. He'd *really* wanted to find Dustin and apologise for yesterday, but he just wasn't there. Thankfully there was a different security guard on duty, too, or he'd have been accosted and warned about wandering the store again. At least he actually had a reason to be there this time!

Aaron pushed off and began slowly pedalling along the road and up towards the woodland that would take him home via the hut that had quickly started to feel like an extension of his house in itself. He shivered a little. It really was starting to get cold, and these roads would soon be an icy death trap to cyclists like him. The sooner he could get into the woods the better.

The leaves had started to rot on the floor of the already badly-defined path through the familiar woodland, and Aaron had to keep stopping to clear leaf-gunk from his tyres and chain every few minutes or so. Eventually, however, he reached the hut and slowed his bike to a stop. The cold winds that seemed to swirl around the area in which the hut stood was really doing a number on the old building, and Aaron was *sure* it looked in a worse state than it had when he was here yesterday, but perhaps it was just his imagination.

He scanned around the floor of the hut and found the journal exactly where he'd left it. No new entries, no new replies. Nothing since he'd written in it just 24 hours previously. His heart sank. He'd been so consumed by remorse over the way in which he'd treated Dustin at the shop yesterday, and he had been hoping that X would have some advice, or at the very least forgiveness for him. No such luck.

Sitting on the floor of the hut, Aaron felt defeated. It was freezing cold, and he grabbed his arms for warmth and closed his eyes, leaning back against the dusty brick of the old, abandoned shack. If only there were some kind of sign, something that might help him get further with this investigation. More information about Emma, or some kind of breakthrough about who the killer might be. He felt lost. Powerless. Like a failure.

He sat there for a few minutes, his breathing steady, enjoying the peaceful calm of the situation. Suddenly, however, a forceful gust of cold wind seemed to force its way through the door and push into Aaron like a block of ice. He opened his eyes and gasped. There, on the ceiling of the hut, was chalk-drawn writing, How long had it been there? Was it new, or had he just not looked up properly before now? He quickly stood up, right on tiptoes, and tried to make out what the words said.

'How many more are going to die? Will I be next? Save us.'

He stepped back, dumbfounded by what he'd just read. He felt dizzy, off-balance. 'Save us' it had said, and Aaron's mind had immediately taken him back to the fog in his dreams, and the screaming voices that had so often woken him up in terror.

He steadied himself in the doorway of the hut, looking down at the ground as he tried to pace his breathing and clear his mind. They were only words, he told himself. They couldn't hurt him. Once he was a little calmer, he took his phone out and snapped a picture of the barely-legible chalk. He'd look at it again later, but for now all he could think about was getting out of there, and getting back home to where it was warm.

The wind was getting stronger as Aaron attempted to cycle back through the path in the woods. It was biting into his face like he imagined a piraña would bite into its prey, slowly twisting his nerve endings and causing him infinitely more pain than he'd expected on this ride home. Next time, he thought to himself, he'd wear a face protector.

He peddled on, seeing the light getting brighter up ahead, indicating that he was near the end of the woods and the start of the flatlands that surrounded the old farmhouse. Breaking into the clearing, his mind was suddenly snapped back into focus. There was a car in the driveway, parked next to his mother's. An old car, and not one he recognised.

Thinking on his feet, he jumped off his bike and wheeled it back through the clearing, hiding it behind the mess of mostly-bare trees at the mouth of the woods. Shedding everything vaguely reflective, he then ran from the clearing to the front of the house, and hid behind one of the untidy shrubs that stood against the mottled white-and-grey wall. There was no window here, so he couldn't peer inside, but he was home earlier than he usually would be so he could stay here and see if the owner of the car would show themselves.

He peered trough the bush at the car. It was a Ford Fiesta, but not one you'd be proud to own by any stretch of the imagination. A bilious green colour, with patches of rust clearly visible around the edges and seams, it looked like an elderly car factory had vomited it into the world some hundred or so years ago. Aaron took out his phone and took another couple of photos. He couldn't make out the entire number plate from where he was, but he took a photo of the few characters he could make out. Opening the browser on his phone, he typed 'what year were T reg cars made' and was surprised to learn it was made in 1999, the same year he was born.

He continued to wait behind the bush, his crouching pose beginning to hurt his already aching knees. He shuffled his feet, trying to stretch a little without giving his position away to anyone that might be watching. After what felt like an hour, but was more like 15 minutes, he heard voices and the front door opened.

"Thank you so much for coming, dear." He heard his mother's voice, filled with gratitude and a hint of sadness. "It must be so hard."

He saw two people leave the house, his mother shielding the view of the unknown benefactor of her kindness. They were tall, but between the bush, the angle at which he was crouched, and his mother, he couldn't really make out who or what they were.

"You take care, keep smiling okay?"

She leaned in and planted a kiss on the cheek of the faceless person, and walked back into the house. Taking the opportunity to shift his body a little, Aaron managed to turn himself around a little and could now see the windscreen of the car, whose door he heard close with a rust-muffled bang. Craining his neck, he tried desperately to see who was inside the ancient vehicle, but all he could see from this angle was a t-shirt and a phone get attached to a mount on the dashboard.

Hands gripped the steering wheel. The engine started. Running out of time to react, Aaron opened up the camera on his phone once again and started snapping pictures. The car started pulling back, and suddenly Aaron could see the driver more clearly— they were facing backwards, watching out of the rear window as the car reversed, but at this point it was clear that it was a man. A tall one, with shaggy hair. Suddenly the driver's head snapped back round to face the front, giving Aaron a totally unobscured view of who he was before the car turned and sped off down the dirt-track driveway that led to the farmhouse.

Aaron dropped his phone, in a state of shock for the second time that afternoon.

It was Dustin.

## Chapter Seventeen

"Remind me what we're doing this for again, Devvo?"

"Property developers, innit. Whole area's going to be flats or something."

"Always the bloody same. What were all these little buildings and sheds for, anyway?

"Used to be a railway that ran through here, back in Victorian times. Yonks ago, mate. 'Bout time someone tore 'em down. If it wan't for this bloody public footpath we'd just be able to cordon the whole place off."

"Does anyone even come through here?

"Dog walkers? Teenagers wanting a place to shag? There's a house up that way, and some fields and flood plains, so I guess enough people to make it worth protecting."

"Not going to be coming here for privacy once the diggers move in, are they?

"Heh, probably won't stop them."

Ste and Devvo, clad in heavy orange work clothes, were hauling metal fencing off the back of the pick-up truck that they'd driven carefully through the woods. Marking the side of the barely-visible mud track that constituted the public right of way with bright yellow spray paint, this was one of the simpler jobs their two-person firm had been contracted by the local council to carry out.

"Mark the path, put up the fence. Is that really it?"

"Afraid so, Ste."

"No demolition, chainsawing trees, or explosions of any kind?"

"Not unless you want me to dock your pay, you nutter."

"But it's been ages since we burned anything."

"You worry me."

The pair worked with well-practised efficiency. While Ste was technically still an apprentice, Devvo tended to see him as a reasonable—if not significantly younger—equal. Other than his vague tendency to want to start fires and burn things, that was.

"Alright, you put the stumps down, I'll slot the fencing in."

The fencing they were putting up was, in Devvo's expert opinion, going to last about five minutes. It was the cheap, flimsy, easy to blow over stuff that didn't interconnect or bolt together or anything. He'd warned the council that they'd end up spending more in the long run than if they just sprung for the more expensive fencing, but hey. Their money, their decision.

"Look at this hut, Dev. It's crumbling, but could we use it to fix one of the fence panels to, make it a bit more sturdy?"

"Looks good Ste, grab the sledge hammer and some of those ceramic fixers from the truck."

Devvo inspected the hut that Ste had brought his attention to. It looked old, far older than he'd have expected it to be and have it still be standing. The flat roof seemed vaguely intact, too. He peered inside—nothing obvious, no people at least. Some writing on the ceiling, but then what abandoned building *didn't* end up covered in graffiti. Ste wandered back with the largest of the hammers they carried and some sharp looking metal slugs.

"Stand back then, hold the panel in place."

Ste placed one of the metal slugs over the fencing, pointing at the wall of the hut, and took a few steps back. The slugs looked like giant staples, designed to penetrate brick and stone and hold things to them firmly. They needed a good whack, though, so Ste stood with his legs apart and got his body ready for the swing.

"Cover your eyes, here I go!"

Ste expertly swung the heavy wooden handle of the dull, grey metal of the hammer toward the slug, following through with all the muscle he could muster. The slug, just millimetres from the wall, hung ready to receive the blow and penetrate the brick ahead of it.

Time slowed down for Ste, as the lumbering, elephantine head of the hammer hit the slug and it bore its way into the wall. Only, it didn't. As the slug began to penetrate the brick it crumbled to dust, showing its age in one final act. The wall around it began to crack, too, as the hammer continued its destructive path through the hole that had just been made by the crumbling brick.

Dust started rising as the bricks around the newly-made hole started to disintegrate and turn to dust. This structure had been unstable, left alone for years until the fateful blow from the hammer.

"Get out the way!" Ste managed to yell, as he dropped the hammer and ran backwards away from the hut. Devvo, who had been holding the fencing in place, dropped it and took off at a pace across the path and toward the woodland opposite the hut. The pair watched the scene unfold in front of them, time almost standing still.

Cracks continued to emanate from the original hole, but now more was going on. Where Devvo had dropped the fence panel, another brick had started to give way. And another. The two separate reactions from either side of the hut continued for what can only have been milliseconds before meeting, and then came an almighty crash.

The flat roof of the hut started to give way, pulling itself apart as the hundred-year-old brick supporting it started to give way. The roof's collapse only served to further accelerate the crumbling of the brickwork, and within a matter of seconds the hut had been reduced to a pile of rubble and a few blocks of wood.

"Err… Sorry."

"You're lucky it was slated to be demolished anyway, you muppet."

"I'll go get the accident report book…"

Ste stalked off to the truck, and Devvo surveyed the scene in front of him. It had been an accident, but he probably should have predicted it and not let Ste try to fix the fencing to it. Oh well, at least they were putting the fence up anyway, they could easily cordon off the area and make it safe. Devvo sighed, kicked the few bits of brick that had fallen onto the path back into the pike of rubble, and waited for Ste to get back with the paperwork.

He *hated* the paperwork.

## Chapter Eighteen

Aaron awoke with a start. He looked over at his alarm clock and, on seeing that the time was 10:42, sat bolt upright. While he might not have always been thrilled about school, he was never usually late like this! Why hadn't his Mum woken him up?

He bunched up the duvet and swung his legs out of bed. Ready to jump up and throw on his uniform, when another thought suddenly came to him. He checked his phone, looking underneath the time— now 10:43—to the date. It was Sunday. Aaron swung his legs back round onto the bed and let his head fall to the pillow. Idiot, he thought to himself, as he closed his eyes and pulled the duvet back over himself to reclaim some of the warmth from within.

He'd been getting himself confused about little things more and more recently. Tiny, insignificant things, but they'd all started to add up and had left him feeling vaguely uneasy. He'd put the milk away in the cupboard yesterday instead of in the fridge, tried to ride off without unlocking his bike, taken the wrong day's text books into school… small stuff that led him to one big problem: he was distracted.

Since his plethora of disturbing discoveries last week, he'd been entirely unable to focus or concentrate on anything. It hadn't been helped by the fact he'd spent all of yesterday in bed feeling under the weather, but even then he was sure that he was stressing himself out over all things journal related.

He wanted to go back and see if X had written any more but still didn't feel much like leaving his bed, let alone his house. He'd  check on his way to school tomorrow, he thought to himself, as he curled up in his duvet and let himself drift off again.

He heard his phone beep, opened his eyes again, and rolled over. He was sure he'd only just closed his eyes again, but the clock now read 11:55. "You're so lazy" he said to himself, as he picked up his phone and looked at the notification.

'New Twitter post by @JustinTerrobang: "Loving the emmatal & mushro…" URL https:// www.twitt….'

Aaron groaned. Another useless notification. Nothing useful had come of that search alert since Dustin's Instagram post, and he was starting to think that disabling the damned thing might be better than getting all of these notifications. I mean, why couldn't this Justin guy learn how to spell his favourite cheeses properly?

Realising that his bladder was giving him a not-so-subtle nudge in the direction of the bathroom, he got out of bed and walked over to the bedroom door. He felt a little dizzy. After the pill he took a few nights previously, he hadn't taken any more, and it seemed to have a worse affect on him this time around. Shaking his head, he looked for something to cover his nakedness. He didn't really like wearing his dressing gown, but threw it on and headed down the stairs to the bathroom one floor below.

\* \* \*

Magda heard hear son stirring upstairs and looked at the clock on the living room wall. Almost mid-day. He really did need to catch up on his sleep, she thought to herself, as she got out of the chair and headed towards the door. She reached for the remote and paused the TV show she was watching, and stuck her head around the door to call up the stairs.

"Good morning, sleepy! Do you want anything to eat?

No reply came.

"Aaron?"

"Mum, I'm in the bathroom. Not right now thanks."

"Okay, Kleine! Sorry."

She threw the remote over to the sofa at the other side of the room and made her way from the living room into the kitchen. It had been a couple of hours since her last cup of tea, and he she made one for Aaron he'd probably drink it… if he came downstairs!

*  *  *

Aaron stumbled back into his room, threw off the dressing gown, and got back into bed. Sure, he should probably get up, but his head felt fuzzy and he didn't exactly have much else to do. He needed some time to think about everything he'd seen and experienced this week, from the Dustin encounter in the shop to seeing him leave his house after meeting with his Mum. How did they even know each other, anyway?

A knock came from his door, and he quickly covered up his mostly-naked body with his duvet.

"Come in, Mama."

"I made you some tea, I thought you might like it. I was going to leave it downstairs for you, but heard you come back up to your room."

"Thanks. Come to think of it, I could use a drink."

"Shall I just put it down over here?"

"Huh? Oh, yeah, thanks."

Aaron watched as his mother put the drink down on the side and looked over at him, her head to one side like a curious puppy.

"You doing okay, Lammkotelett?"

"Mum, it doesn't work if you try and use English expressions in German."

"But I always found it so cute when parents called their children lambchop,"

"I know, Mum, but in German it just sounds… weird."

"So ein Misthaufen!"

"I'm just feeling a bit under the weather, I'll be fine by tomorrow I'm sure. Thanks for the tea, it's great."

"Okay, I'll leave you to get some peace… *Lammkotelett.*"

Aaron groaned aloud at his mother's deliberate use of German where it ought not to be used and she left the room, and began to pull the heavy wooden door closed behind her. He'd been thinking about whether he should ask his mother about how she knew Dustin, and suddenly, Aaron realised that this could be his chance to get some answers.

"Mum?"

The door stopped closing.

"Yes?"

"Can I talk to you about something?"

His mother pushed the door back open, and walked back into the room, the puzzled expression on her face making it seem almost more lined than it usually was.

"Of course, Kleine, what's on your mind?"

"It's just… I still feel bad about the way I spoke to you at lunch the other day. I was angry and frustrated. I just can't work it out, are you keeping things from me, or when you said you *used* to know someone called Emma  it was someone totally different to the one I was thinking of."

Magda sighed. "Yes, totally different, she was just an old friend, someone from years ago."

"Oh, okay. I just… never mind."

"Come on, Kleine. No point keeping it in."

"I just wondered if it as the same Emma that Dustin knew, thats all."

"Dustin?" Magda's voice suddenly took on a tremor that Aaron picked up on. "Who's that? Oh, didn't he used to go to your school?"

"You know who Dustin is, Mama."

"I don't think so dear, only vaguely. Anyway, I'm sure its a common name."

"I guess so."

Aaron was trying to play dumb, in spite of the overwhelming urge he had to yell there and then about having seen Dustin and her talking outside the house. He counted his breathing and thought carefully about his next question, but before he could find the words his mother spoke again.

"Is that all, dear?"

"No. I mean… I don't know. Do you… do you know anyone called X?"

There was a pause of several seconds in which the words seemed to hang in the air. Magda Grayling tensed up, making her already pained expression seem oddly menacing and imposing. Lost for words, the pair looked at each other, both seemingly desperate not to reveal their true feelings about the conversation they found themselves in.

Slowly, Magda let out a long breath.

"Don't be silly, dear. Nobody is called X. Maybe you're getting a fever. Anyway, I have things to go and do so if you don't have anything important to talk to me about I'll just head down and get on…"

"Okay, mama." Aaron replied through clenched teeth. "See you."

As the door closed behind her and the sounds of her shuffling down the stairs grew quieter, Aaron let out a breath himself and said, mostly to the closed door, "liar."

Shaking with anger, he jumped out of bed and walked over to the desk on which Magda had placed his tea. Pulling out the chair from underneath the slightly flimsy, home-built structure, he sat down and reached into the drawer for a pencil.

He pulled over a piece paper, wrote the name 'Emma' in the middle of it, and drew a circle around it.

"Right" he said aloud as he drew. "So Dustin and Emma, connected *there*."

He had written Dustin's name on the sheet with a similar circle around it, and connected the two circles together with a line.

"And then there's X"

He did the same for X, and drew a line connecting him to Dustin.

"And then Mum is in here. Now that I know I can't

trust her, I've got to assume she's connected to them both."

He drew lines between his mother and both Dustin and Emma.

"And then there's me. And I seem to know everyone except Emma, but everyone except X seem to be bloody liars."

He drew lines from him to his mother, to Dustin, and to X.

"I don't get it. If Mum knows Dustin and Emma, and Dustin and Emma are together, or were together, then how come I've never met Emma? And what does X really have to do with any of them, other than knowing Dustin and wanting to investigate her disappearance?"

He sat staring at the piece of paper, trying to make sense of it. It was starting to feel like there was some kind of conspiracy against him, with all these people seeming to know more than he did, and his mother now outright lying about things. Only the paranoid create conspiracy theories, he thought to himself, but what was he meant to think when people were being dishonest right to his face?

Feeling frustrated by the whole situation, Aaron

picked up the piece of paper and screwed it tightly into a ball in his hands. Aiming for the bin on the far wall by the sink, he arced his arms and threw as hard as he could. The balled up piece of paper flew through the air, entirely missing the bin and landing in the sink.

"Typical."

He got up from the chair, stretched his aching legs, and downed the remainder of his tea. Striding back over toward his bed, he picked up his phone from the bedside table, unplugged the charger, and opened up the photo that he took of the chalk writing in the hut last week.

The handwriting didn't match with the neatness of X's usual scratchings in the journal, and it didn't really look like anyone else's writing he knew, including his own. So who wrote it? And why was it just like the words that the voices in his dream seemed to scream at him?

He threw on his dressing gown again and headed down to the bathroom to take a shower. Maybe that would help him clear his head.

## Chapter Nineteen

It was dark. Aaron was in bed, but he couldn't move or speak. He tried to scream  but it was like his vocal chords had just disappeared, and all he could manage was a heavy breath as he pushed air from his lungs in an attempt to make a sound. He couldn't feel anything other than the weight of his own body. This was definitely a different kind of dream than the last few.

He lay there, his eyes trying to focus in the dark, reaching out for any kind of shape or change in the blackness. Slowly, feeling started to return to his numb hands and back and he realised that, rather than being in his bed, he was lying on something uneven, cold, and wet. He tried to feel around with his hands, but could only manage to move his fingers a little, sliding them unsteadily up and down whatever surface he was lying on.

 The feeling was familiar, and he continued to move his fingers as his brain tried to process the sensations that his nerve endings were sending him. Mud. It felt like earthy mud. As he lay there, he slowly started to feel sensation returning to the rest of his body, as if someone were going along his limbs slowly re-activating his sense of touch millimetre by agonising millimetre.

He was lying on the ground somewhere, he deduced. Somewhere wet, not that he could feel any rain, but the mud was fresh and rich and plentiful. He tried to move his hand up to his face, but the blackness around him was so complete that while he felt like he'd achieved it, he couldn't actually see his hand, or the rest of his body at all.

Time passed. He wasn't sure how much time, but he guessed it had been around ten minutes. He tried to close his eyes and count the seconds, but he seemed to be entirely unable to focus on anything. Had it been ten minutes, ten seconds, or ten hours? The more he thought about it all, the more he second guessed himself. Did time matter right now?

As he lay there continuing to contemplate where he might be and why, he noticed something in the distance. Or, perhaps, right in front of him. The darkness had so far been so all-encompassing, he could tell distance about as well as he could count time. And yet, something was definitely stirring in front of him. After a few seconds of his eyes trying and failing to adjust he closed them, attempting to heighten his other senses and see if he could hear anything, or detect any vibrations or disturbances in the air around him.

Nothing.

He found himself wondering whether this was a dream, or whether it was actually real this time. Either way, this was an experience unlike any previous dream, and like no time awake he could remember in his almost 18 years of life. The environment around him was totally foreign, and the pure darkness was overpowering in its numb emptiness.

The shape, or shadow, or whatever it was was still flirting with his peripheral vision. It looked like a wisp of fog, barely visible, somehow illuminated in this forest of darkness while nothing else was. He could see that it was slowly it growing larger, becoming a very visible yet almost indistinguishable smudge roaming around in the air. Was it just him? No, it couldn't be.Whatever it was, it was definitely getting bigger, or closer, as he watched. Before long, Aaron felt the air around him grow colder, the first feeling of atmospheric presence he'd had in this place since he had found himself in this place.

Air began to wash over him, at first like a light breeze, but steadily growing into a roaring that blew at his face and body. He could hear it now as well as feel it, like a hurricane approaching. He closed his eyes to shield them from the intensity of the cold, hard wind.

And then, it stopped.

He opened his eyes to find the grey slither of fog was right up close to him. Again he tried to speak, but no words would come. Suddenly, filling his ears, his brain, his heart, his entire being, a voice spoke to him

"Keep looking, Aaron."

As the words came, so did the wind. It was like the breath of an almighty cloud, hollering the words at him from its icy interior.

"Keep looking. You will find it again."

The voice stopped, and a bright overpowering light

suddenly erupted around him. He closed his eyes, needing to adjust to the sudden influx of light. The wind had gone, leaving him lying in the mud. Slowly opening his eyes again, he realised that he was surrounded by bright fog, just like in his previous dreams.

He looked down at his body and realised that he was indeed lying in mud. Sitting up, his body now free from whatever hold the darkness had on him, he wiped the mud from his legs and his arms. He was *covered* in it, head to toe.

Before he had much time to gather his thoughts, he felt the ground beneath him gently rumble. He placed his hands flat down to get a better feel, and it grew slightly more intense. He could hear it now, like an earthquake approaching from the distance. He got up, ready to run away from it, but the ground around him was now shaking violently and he fell to the floor with a wet thud.

Suddenly, he felt the ground beneath him give way. He was falling, white fog all around him, rumbling noise continuing to fill his ears. He could see something in the distance, beneath him. A dark shape rapidly approaching. He started to scream, his body in free-fall as he hurtled towards what he now knew was something solid.

And he awoke. Drenched in sweat once again, he sat up in bed and looked around him. Same old room, same old place, but somehow a very different dream than anything he'd had before.

What the *hell* did it mean?

## Chapter Twenty

Aaron threw his hoodie on over his blazer and sat on his bike as he pulled his phone out and checked the time. Seven thirty. Far too early to need to leave for school, but he just hadn't been able to go back to sleep after the dream he'd had last night. He was feeling worse than he had felt since he'd stopped taking his tablets, too. Not so much dizzy, but a little feverish. Like his head was just a little out of step with reality.

It was his second to last week of school this term, and he could do without a fuzzy head right now. He couldn't wait for the break from school to start, giving him the time to do some cycling for fun, to work more on his university applications, and to really get to the bottom of the investigation with X. Shoving his phone back in his pocket, he pushed off from the side of the house and headed toward the clearing in the woods that would take him back past the hut and towards school for the day.

The sky was still dark as Aaron pushed down on the pedals, the wheels of his bike picking up sodden earth as it slowly churned and turned to mud beneath him. As he passed the clearing and headed into the woods even the cloud-obscured glow of moonlight and impending sunrise faded, leaving his bike lights the only source of illumination in the dark mass of trees in front of him. Noticing some strange markings on the ground ahead of him, Aaron stopped his bike and slowly unclipped his front bike light from the mount that held it to the handlebar. Sliding off his bike, he lent down to investigate.

It looked like someone had been spray painting the earthen floor of the path, spraying yellow lines along the edge of it, marking it out like a builder before starting work on a road. He shone his torch over to the other side of the path and saw the same markings, stretching out along the path, roughly equidistant to one another.

Shining his bike light into the distance, something vaguely metallic seemed to be reflecting back in his direction. He stood up and tried to strain his eyes to see what it was, but couldn't quite make it out yet. Getting back onto his bike, he reattached the light and started to cycle slowly forwards, down the familiar path that had suddenly inherited unfamiliar characteristics.

The object reflecting his bike light grew closer, and he once again slowed his bike to a stop. There, at the side of the path, was a metal fence panel. Looking ahead he could see that the fencing continued into the distance on both sides of him, closing it in. It was like someone had cordoned off the woodland around the path, protecting it from passers by.

A thought suddenly crossed his mind, and he set off at a faster pace down the now-enclosed pathway. The hut—it was just off the path, would there be a piece of fence in front of it? If so, how easy would it be to remove? Aaron had planned to spend some time investigating the journal this morning on his way in, and was suddenly filled with dread that somehow he might have to dismantle a fence to get to it.

The reality he was faced with was far worse.

Aaron dropped his bike to the ground and stood, mouth open, in a state of shock. In front of him, where the hut normally stood, was not only a fence panel but a pile of rubble. His brain took a few seconds to process the scene in front of him before snapping back into action. Reaching down to once again liberate the light from the front of his bike, he shone it through the thin metal grille of the fence and illuminated the scene of devastation that now lay before him.

The hut had been completely decimated. Bits of timber from the roof jutted upward like arms reaching out for salvation, while all around were the remnants of brickwork and dust from what had obviously been a catastrophic collapse. What had happened here?

Aaron was in shock, and the buzzing in his head he'd felt since waking up was getting worse, making him dizzy and nauseous. He'd cycled past this hut for years before paying it any attention, but over the past few months he'd become attached to it, its dusty walls his only connection to X, Emma, and the murder investigation he had been thrust into the middle of. He put his fingers through the mesh of the fence and pulled at it, seeing if he could move it out of the way easily. It wobbled and swayed, but so did every other panel that side of the path. If he pulled it over, he'd be trapped underneath it.

He pushed the fence panel upwards, and realised that it wasn't fixed down into the heavy rubber holdings that lined the woodland floor. He found the strength from his anger and upset, letting out a small roar as he pulled upwards and pushed hard, throwing the flimsy metal fence panel off to the side and into the deeper foliage to the left of what used to be the hut.

Free from the fencing that obstructed his access to the now-ruined hut, Aaron moved closer to the pile of rubble and shone his torch over it. Falling to his knees, he began to weep. There was nothing left of the hut save rubble and dust, and it felt to Aaron like someone had removed one of his arms or legs. It hurt.

Reeling, almost hyperventilating, he begun to thrash around in the rubble, hunting through the pieces of brick and stone for the thing he'd come here to see.

"Journal… must… be… here… somewhere."

He searched through his tears, his school uniform now caked in brick dust and mud, as the sun started to rise and the sky lightened a little. No sign of the journal, no sign of X. Nothing. He threw himself atop the pile of rubble, shivering from the cold and the dizziness in his head, heaving with tears, collapsing into a muddy, crying ball.

After a few minutes his tears began to subside, and Aaron opened his eyes. How could this have happened? Who did it? And where had the journal gone? He looked down at his clothes and realised that he was in no state to go to school. What was he supposed to do now? The hut was… gone.

He tried to stand up, but couldn't balance. Crawling, he circled the remains of the hut. Shining his torch on all he could, he took his phone from his pocket and started to take photos. There were bits of brick *everywhere*, and it would take Aaron a *long* time to photograph them all. He stopped on all fours, ready to give up, when a set of bricks against a nearby tree caught his attention.

Shining the light over to them, it looked as if something had been written on them using the same chalk that he had seen in the hut a few days previously. He dragged himself closer, crouching down under the thick branches of the tree and focussing his bike light on the three bricks that sat at the base. The bricks were wet, clearly from recent rainfall, but the words were still clear. And familiar.

"Keep looking Aaron."

He rolled onto the floor beside the bricks, his head pounding. It was starting to get brighter around him, but through the thick clouds the morning light seemed dirty, somehow tainted. A rumble of thunder broke the silence, and rain began to fall in thick droplets, penetrating the trees and finding their way to the floor on which Aaron was now curled up, clutching his head, breathing heavily while he tried to hang on to his sanity.

The cold rain started to penetrate his hoodie and school trousers, and he begun to shiver harder. He rolled onto his back and ran his hands along the ground beneath him. It was earthy, muddy. Familiar. Screwing his eyes up tight, he let out an almighty scream—all of the angst and frustration, confusion, and hurt flowing from his lungs up through his vocal chords and out into the air around him. Birds fled from nearby trees, the only response to the pain that was writhing on the ground beneath them.

He closed his eyes and, exhausted as he lay there in the mud and dust and rain, lost consciousness.

## Chapter Twenty-One

Swish. Scrape. Swish. Scrape. Swish. Scrape. Click click, click click, click click.

Dustin indicated left and turned slowly, the sound of his indicator almost lost in the maelstrom of wind and rain around him. The only thing louder than the heavy rain mercilessly hitting his windscreen was the sound of the broken windscreen wiper blade slowly scoring a scratch into the cold hard glass at the front of his dad's old car.

He was struggling to keep focussed. The journey to work was usually one he could do on autopilot given how much time he spent there, but the weather today was such that if he didn't concentrate to extremes he might well end up crashing into a wall, flying off a corner, or hitting someone or something because he couldn't stop in time.

The old green Fiesta crept along the small roads that made up his journey around the old farm and woodlands that stood between Trenton and his job in Meriville. He turned the corner that took him the rest of the way to the shop, and peered through half-closed eyes out of the window to try and make out any traffic or terrain features.

He could see something black on the side of the road up ahead, like a clump of... *something*. He swerved into the right hand lane to avoid it, craning his neck for a closer look as he went by. Jesus, he thought, that's a person! Slamming on his brakes Dustin skidded forward scarily for a few moments before coming to a stop. Putting the car into reverse, he pulled up behind the human bump in the road and got out of the car to investigate.

The rain was intense, and Dustin's work shirts was soaked within seconds. He walked around the car and stopped in front of the figure hunched over in the road, conscious and crying, face obscured by a hood.

"Hello? Is everything okay? God... Emma? Is that you?"

The figure spoke, its voice raspy and shivering.

"It's Aaron. Leave me alone."

Dustin walked over to where Aaron was sitting and crouched in front of him.

"Dude, you're soaking wet, you're covered in mud, and you're crying. What part of that tells me that I should leave you alone?"

"Get *out* of here, Dustin!" Aaron said with anger in his voice. He flailed out his arms in front of him pushing Dustin over, making him fall onto the wet surface of the road. Aaron looked shocked.

"I'm... I'm sorry."

Dustin got up grabbed him by the arm, and dragged him to his feet. He looked *awful*, his skin white, his hair matted to his face. He was covered in mud and grit, and soaked to his core. He felt freezing cold to the touch. He released Aaron's arm and the boy begun to fall forward, clearly lacking the strength and balance to stand up on his own two feet.

"I'm taking you to the hospital"

"No…" Aaron replied weakly. "No hospital. Just home."

"But I really think you should…"

"Home." Aaron interrupted, and promptly fell forward into Dustin, seeming to lose consciousness.

"Alright, buddy. I'll take you home."

He opened up the passenger door of the car and, haphazardly throwing his arm around Aaron's shoulder, eased him down into he seat. He grabbed a leg—muddy, smelly, covered in grit and dirt, and fling it into the passenger side footwell. The other leg followed, and Dustin pulled the seatbelt over the unconscious Aaron, plugged it into the holder the other side of him, and closed the car door.

Dustin, by now soaking himself, walked quickly around the car and jumped back in to the drivers seat. Reversing back into the spot he'd just picked Aaron up from, he spun his car around and headed in the opposite direction to work, back toward the old farm lands and Aaron's home.

Pulling up the driveway, Dustin noticed with some relief that Magda's car wasn't there. She'd surely take him to the hospital, but Aaron was fervently against that. Looking over into the passenger seat he could see that Aaron was now shivering. He had to get him warmed up and safe, fast.

Fumbling around in Aaron's hoodie pocket, Dustin found his keys and opened the front door. He only vaguely knew the layout of the house, but having used the toilet here before he knew that there was a shower in the bathroom on the first floor. Returning to the car, Dustin put his arms around his barely-conscious friend and hoisted him up onto his feet. After a few seconds of awkward experimenting, Dustin managed to wrap both of Aaron's arms around his shoulders and lift him against his back.

Kicking the front door closed behind him he hauled Aaron up the stairs, dripping water and mud on the floor as he went. Getting him into the bathroom, Dustin placed him gently on the side of the bath and lowered him into the tub.

"Okay, the easiest way to warm you up is a shower."

He turned on the shower that hung above the bath, took the shower head from its holding, and pointed it at the plug hole. Checking the temperature was warm but not boiling, he began to move the shower head up and down Aaron's shivering figure, washing the mud from his clothes and slowly warming him up.

"Aaron, you're going to have to get those clothes off if you don't want to catch hypothermia or something."

Aaron slowly started to move his shivering hands to the zip on his hoodie, but utterly failed to actually pull the zip down to release it.

"Seriously? Dude, this isn't going to be easy for me. Seeing you naked isn't… it's just… okay, just don't die alright?"

Dustin unzipped the hoodie and began the process of removing Aaron's clothing as clinically as he could. His school uniform was soaking. The blazer was so sodden it was likely ruined, the shirt was stained with mud, and the trousers were jet black with how much water they was retaining. Throwing the clothes into the corner of the room, he kept the shower head pointing at Aaron, letting the warm water flow over his skinny, shaking frame.

Slowly the shivering slowed, leaving Aaron naked and breathing heavily in the bathtub. Dustin turned off the shower and gently shook his friends shoulders to see if he was conscious.

"Hey, Aaron? You awake there buddy?"

"Unnngghhh" came the muffled response.

Conscious but not quite with it, thought Dustin.

"Okay, I'm going to have to get you out of the bath and dry now, so just stay calm."

Allowing the last of the water to drain away, Dustin grabbed a towel from the rail near the bath and threw it over Aaron. He reached his arms around under his back and pulled upwards, sitting him up in the bath with the towel covering his front. He moved around to the back of Aaron, wrapped his arms around his wet body, and pulled him up and out of the bath completely.

He wasn't able to stand, but could support his weight as Aaron leant him against the wall and started to dry him off. His hair wasn't clean, but was considerably less dirty than it had been earlier. The rest of him seemed to have cleaned up well, but he was looking a peaky-red colour and didn't feel like he was retaining much of the heat he'd got from the shower.

Finishing off the drying process, Dustin realised how wet he still was and pulled off his work shirt and jeans leaving him in a plain-white t-shirt and his tartan patterned underwear. He reached for a towel, and wrapped it around himself.

"Your room is upstairs, right? On the top floor?"

Aaron nodded and made some vague noises of agreement.

"Okay, hold on tight once I get hold of you, I'll carry you up."

Dustin once again got Aaron into a hold over his back, grabbing his arms as they came over his shoulders. Hoisting him up, he could feel Aaron's cold body against his through the thin layer of his t-shirt. He needed to get warm again, and fast.

Heaving Aaron up the stairs, Dustin reached his bedroom door and thrust open with his foot. The room smelled like teenager, but wasn't anywhere as untidy as a regular teenagers room would be. He spotted Aaron's bed at the far side of the room and, pulling back the duvet, slid Aaron inside. He tucked him into the duvet tightly, sat down on the floor beside the bed, and let out a long sigh.

This was not how he imagined his day going.

Dustin walked back down to the bathroom and surveyed the scene in front of him. There was mud covering many of the surfaces and the shabbily-tiled walls, and a large wet spot on the floor where the pile of their collective wet clothes were sat. He'd been in such a hurry to get Aaron warmed up he hadn't really thought about the mess he'd been making.

Peering out the door and down the stairs, he was somewhat relieved that there weren't mud stains on the carpet or walls going down the stairs. He looked around the bathroom for a cleaning cloth and, finding one under the sink, set about wiping the bath and the sides. The last thing he wanted was an earful about causing a mess in someone else's bathroom!

As he cleaned, he heard a text-message alert tone coming from the pile of wet clothes in the corner. He rummaged around the pile and found Aaron's still-sopping-wet school trousers, and rummaged for the pocket from which the noise seemed to be emanating.

Before long, Dustin had found Aaron's phone, thankfully still working in spite of the onslaught of water it had experienced over the past few hours. There was a text message from 'Mum' showing up on the slightly wet screen, but no preview of the message. Dustin tried to swipe at it to get it to show, but the phone was locked.

He slid the phone into the waistband of his boxer shorts for safe keeping, and continued to clean up the mess he had made in the bathroom. Once it was more or less acceptable, Dustin picked up the pile of wet clothes and one-by-one he wrung them all out in the bath.

Satisfied that the clothes no longer posed a massive drip hazard, he balled them up and walked back up the stairs to Aaron's room. Throwing the clothes—both Aaron's and his—into the washing basket that sat in the corner, he signed and looked over at his friend breathing deeply in the bed at the other side of the room. Dustin moved over to him and placed his hand on his forehead. Thankfully, he seemed to be warming up.

"Aaron, there's a text here from your Mum. What do you want to do about it?"

A hand appeared from under the duvet, thumb extended. Dustin held out the phone and watched as Aaron placed his finger on the home button and, on recognising his finger print, it unlocked. The hand disappeared again, and Dustin took that as permission for him to read the message.

'School phoned. You weren't at registration. What is going on? I saw you leave this morning!'

Dustin looked over at Aaron, who looked like he was starting to breathe easier, and started tapping out a reply.

'Sorry Mum. I felt really sick so I came home. In bed now.'

He hit send, and saw immediately that Magda was typing a reply.

'What kind of sick? Did you come off your bike again?'

Dustin suddenly realised that Aaron would probably have been on his bike this morning, yet it was not with him when he picked him up. Had he had a bike accident, maybe? Or did someone try and take his bike from him? He tapped out another reply:

'Not really sure, bit confused. Need to sleep now.'

The next reply came through in seconds.

'You're taking your medication, right? Be home in an hour.'

Dustin realised that he couldn't stay there and explain his presence without things looking bad for everyone. He didn't want Magda to think that he'd caused Aaron any harm, or that he'd been spending too much time with him after he'd agreed not to just last week.

He put the phone on the bed next to Aaron and stood up. His jeans would be nowhere near dry enough for him to wear right now. He had spare uniform at work, but he had to get there in just jeans and underwear. Aaron wasn't really the same size as Dustin so he doubted that a pair of his jeans would fit, but maybe if he had jogging bottoms, he thought, then he'd be able to borrow a pair. Opening his wardrobe he immediately spotted some grey jogging bottoms and put them on. A little tight, but fine until he got to work.

Moving back over to the bed, Dustin had an idea. He picked up the still-unlocked phone and opened a new text message. Searching the contact list for anything called 'me' he selected what he hoped was Aaron's own number and began to tap out a message.

'Hey, It's Dustin. Found you next to the woods in a bad way. Brought you home and sorted you out without your Mum knowing anything. Don't tell her I helped. Just get better soon. BTW borrowed some trackies. Long story.'

He locked the phone and placed it gently on the bedside table next to Aaron. Looking down at him, a sudden wave of emotion flooded over Dustin. He leaned down, closed his eyes, and kissed his friend on the forehead. He wasn't sure what had come over him. Straightening back up, he stammered a

couple of times in vague apology, but Aaron seemed
to be sleeping peacefully. Walking away slowly he
left the room, closed the door behind him, and
headed out of the house.

**Chapter Twenty-Two**


Magda arrived home and slowly trudged up the stairs in her familiar heavy-set way of walking. She wasn't sure what to make of the messages from Aaron, and was half expecting to get to his room and find him sat up in bed watching TV, pulling a sick day.

"Aaron, I'm home, can I come in?"

No response.

Magda pushed open the door to find Aaron sleeping in bed, curtains open, as if he had just got home and flopped there. Walking over to him she could see that he'd got undressed, at least on the bit of his top half that was showing, but he seemed well tucked in and wrapped up in his duvet.

"Kleine? Bist du wach?"

Aaron did not respond, but was breathing deeply and calmly. She reached over a touched his forehead.

"You are burning up!"

His temperature was high, and in spite of his peaceful appearance he appeared to have a fever. No wonder he sounded confused in his texts, she thought. He did the right thing by coming home. She shook him a couple of times and managed to get a few noises out of him.

"Mama" he said weakly, opening his eyes momentarily to investigate the source of the shaking before closing them again.

"Are you okay, Aaron?"

"Feel… cold."

"You have a fever, do you remember what happened?"

"No"

"Nothing at all?"

Aaron shook his head and tried to open his eyes again. It looked like he was struggling to stay even this awake. There was a light mist of sweat on his forehead, and he recoiled from her touch. He was clearly quite unwell. Pulling her phone our of her pocket, she dialled 111 and put the phone to hear ear.

"Hello? Yes. I'm calling about my son. Aaron Grayling. ST12 8DG. Yes, he's got a high fever and I'm a bit worried. Should I take him into hospital? Yes, okay. No, I don't see any bruises. I'll check his legs, moment."

Magda lifted the duvet up and checked Aaron's legs for bruises.

"No, no bruises or marks. He seems conscious sometimes and asleep at others. Okay I'll try calling his name now. Aaron? Are you with us?"

"No."

"Well, he said no, which I guess means yes. No, I don't have a thermometer. He is not shivering, no, but he is a bit clammy. I don't think so, let me ask him. Aaron, any bump to the head?"

"No."

"He says no. I have only been home for a few

minutes. I think it must have come on suddenly as he left for school earlier but then came home. Yes, yes he does take medication regularly. Chlorpromazine. Okay, so a doctor will call me back? How long? Okay. And he doesn't need to go to hospital? Okay. I'll make sure he's warm and has some water by him. Thank you."

Magda heard the call disconnect and put the phone back in her pocket. They didn't think it was serious and a doctor would call back to make sure. For now though, she needed to get herself into nursemaid mode. She left the room and headed down the stairs into the kitchen, her usual gait a little quicker.

Sweeping into the kitchen, she filled up the kettle with water, put it on, and started rummaging in the cupboard above it.

"Get some chicken soup out for later, that'll help him feel better. Where's that nice tea he likes?" she started muttering to herself as she pulled tins and boxes from the cupboard. The kettle boiled, and she got out two tea mugs. She was always so good at caring for her son when he was sick, she thought, She hadn't had a chance to do this in years. Just as she was pouring water atop the tea bags, her phone rang.

"Hello? Yes this is Aaron's Mum. Magda Grayling. No, no, my husband was English. Yes that's right, a fever. No, but it felt like he was burning up. Yes, he managed to answer my questions a little but just looked like he needed to sleep. Oh, I don't know. No, I haven't seen his urine. Yes, I'll make sure he drinks water. Is tea okay too? He always loves tea to make him feel better. Okay. So you don't think he needs to go to hospital? See how he is in twenty-four hours, okay. And then? Call you, okay. Thank you, doctor. Okay. Goodbye."

"Well," she said out loud to herself, "it looks like a day and a night of house rest for us both!"

She busied herself with the tea and surveyed the plethora of tins and cans in front of her. There was plenty here to make him feel better, she thought to herself. Scanning around, her eye was drawn to the door that led from the kitchen to the conservatory.

"No bike?"

She looked through the door and realised that Aaron's bike was indeed missing. How did he get home? Where was his bike? Still at school? Magda scratched her scalp as she wandered aloud.

"What happened, Aaron? Were you just too sick to ride home? Or did you come off your bike after all?"

She shook her head wearily, sighed as she turned back to the counter, and dutifully and went back to making the tea.

## Chapter Twenty-Three

Dustin walked up the unfamiliar woodland path that led from the town to the farmland on which Aaron and Magda Grayling lived. Clutching a thick coat to him, he grimaced at the cold as he slowly put one foot in front of the other, scanning the world around him as he went.

He wasn't even sure what colour Aaron's bike was, but when Magda called and asked him if he'd go out and search for it he found himself agreeing before he could think otherwise. What was he thinking? Getting involved *at all* was a bad idea, given how keen he was to hide his part in having got Aaron home safely the other day. Had Aaron even seen his message yet?

He scanned around, turning on the head torch he'd found in the boot of his dad's old car and shining through the metal fencing that sat along the sides of the path. What was Aaron doing out here that led to him being in the state he was in when he picked him up at the side of the road? Didn't he *always* cycle this way? Perhaps he met someone—or some thing —that did that to him.

He kept walking forward, looking out for anything that could resemble a bike. So far, all he'd found was the metal fence that had clearly only recently been erected, and a few odd bits of brick and stone. He found his mind wandering to the events two days previous, when he'd had to place his friend in the shower and get him warm. It was an intense experience, over before he'd really had a chance to analyse it. Now that he thought back, he was scared and worried for what might be happening to Aaron. His mother had said that he was getting better, but if that was true then why was he in such a state?

He spotted something up ahead and broke into a jog, the torchlight bobbing as he moved quickly forward. He came to a stop and moved his head around to illuminate the area—revealing a break in the fencing, a pile of rubble, and Aaron's bike, seemingly thrown into the undergrowth at the side of the path.

It was like something out of a bad horror story, Dustin thought as he tried to piece together the picture in front of him. The rubble looked like it was probably once one of the old railway buildings that littered the area but there was no undergrowth around it or near it, making it seem like it had only recently stopped being a building and started being an ex-building.

The missing fence panel was lying just off to the left having clearly been lifted and thrown with some considerable force, and the whole scene looked very much like it had been ransacked or rummaged through. It was Aaron's bike, though, that was the real mystery. It was the other side of the fence to the path, and it looked like it had been dumped in a hurry. Had it been on the path, he could feasibly have crashed or fallen off it, but that can't have been the case given its location. There was a bag still attached to the back of it, adding to the theory that it had been dumped in a hurry, and the bag and bike frame were muddy and wet.

Dustin felt a chill down his spine, and started craning his head around to see the surrounding area. Something was giving him the creeps, and he

didn't much like that feeling. Picking up Aaron's
bike, he wheeled it out of the rubble and
undergrowth and back onto the path. He could hear
a rustling coming from a nearby tree, and his breath
quickened. Time to leave, he thought to himself.

He started walking back in the direction of town,
away from Aaron's house. He was far closer to his
car parked at the town-end of the woods than he
was to the old farm, and he didn't like the idea of
spending longer in these woods than he absolutely
had to. He paused momentarily and the rustling the
trees grew louder. Frozen to the spot, Dustin
wondered what could be making that noise.

Suddenly, it stopped.

He looked around, very much aware of his
breathing and the pounding sound of his own heart
in the silence that now surrounded him. He didn't
dare move. Slowly, cautiously, he moved the bike
forward a little and started to raise one of his legs.
Without making a sound he mounted Aaron's bike
and settled into the padded, soaking wet saddle. As
he did so, he heard a twig snap and the rustling
sound return even louder than before. Startled,
Dustin yelled out in fear, pushed his feet away from
the ground and, finding the peddles, careened off
down the path and away from the noise.

As the sound of Dustin's screams and furious pedalling subsided, a startled fox wandered out of the undergrowth and up to the metal fence. It had smelled the now-rotting food that Aaron had left in his bicycle bag, but now seemed to have lost the scent. Hungry, it trudged back into the undergrowth to see what else it could find.

\*  \*  \*

Folding down the back seats, Dustin sighed. He was still a little freaked out after his speedy escape from the woods, but his breathing was once again steady and, he kept telling himself, it was probably nothing. Besides, he now had bigger fish to fry. Dustin's car was small and he was trying to fit an entire mountain bike inside. He hadn't really had a choice over the car—he couldn't afford one of his own, so he was using his dad's old one. It was great in spite of its age, until you wanted to put something huge in the back of it that was. This was going to be a tough one.

Eventually, Dustin managed to get it in enough to close the car up, even if he'd had to get his passenger seat filthy to do it. He slumped into the driver's seat, started up the engine, and closed the door. It was cold, and he turned the heating up full to try and stave off the shivering he was still experiencing after his close encounter with… whatever it was. He pulled his phone from his pocket and opened up a new text message:

'To: Magda Grayling


Hey, I found Aaron's bike in the woods. No damage, he must have just come off it. Is now a good time to bring it over?'

Dustin made no mention of the rubble, the fence, or the noises he heard in the woods. Magda would just panic if he did, and he wanted to respect Aaron's privacy too. Whatever he was doing out there, he clearly didn't want anyone to know about it.

As he sat waiting for the car to warm up, Dustin was suddenly aware of an awful smell coming from behind him. Craning his neck around, he realised that the bag attached to Aaron's bike was open a little, and what looked like some food was visible through the zip. Reaching back, Dustin grabbed the zipper and pulled the bag shut.

"Ew, whatever's in there is *disgusting*." He said aloud.

Fumbling with the controls, Dustin turned on the car radio. Being a car from the 90s, it had a top quality tape deck built in. Thankfully he'd managed to find a tape adapter online and bought one as soon as he could drive, giving him the somewhat more modern ability to plug his phone into it. Plugging the adapter into the headphone socket he tapped at his phone screen, scrolling down to a playlist called 'Emma' and hit the shuffle button.

The sound of Japanese rock music emanated from the car speakers as Dustin leaned his head back and sighed. Emma had introduced him to this music, and The Gazette was one of her favourite bands. He let the music wash over him, closing his eyes as thoughts of Emma, Aaron, and as the craziness of the past few weeks flickered behind his eyelids like an old-fashioned film, he sung along out loud.

"Tsunagu te to gyaku no te ni wa itsumo shiranai kaori ga shiteru. Iki wa chan to dekiteru no ni kuzure sou ni naru."

The song changed, and Dustin opened his eyes. Looking down at his phone, he realised that he had a new text message.

'Hi Dustin. Yes now is fine. Aaron is still sleeping and has been for a day and a half now. I hope he is okay. Thank you. Magda'

Putting the phone down on the seat beside him, he looked backward out of the rear window and put the car into reverse. "Well, let's get this over with." He said as he turned the wheel and put his foot on the accelerator. The car turned, and Dustin sped off into the night.

\* \* \*

Magda opened the front door and invited Dustin inside. It had only been a week since she had last seen him, but he looked like he hadn't showered for a month. His long hair was matted in places, he had mud on his hands, and his face was unshaven and haggard. And the smell—this couldn't just have been from being out hunting for Aaron's bike.

"Thank you so much for doing this, Dustin. Is his bike okay? I know that he will be happy that it's back here in one piece."

"I'm just glad we found it."

"So where was it? You say it was in the woods?"

"Yeah, I just tracked the journey I know he

normally takes to get from town to here, through that path in the woods, and about a third of the way in from town I found it."

"Just laying there?"

"It… err… yeah. Just off the path, it just looked like he came off it. Nothing else there. Maybe he hit his head and got confused and then walked the rest of the way home, or something."

"This is all very strange. He had such a high fever. It's broken now and he's getting better, but he hasn't woken up yet. The doctor says there's nothing to worry about but still. I… I thought things were finally getting better."

"Better?"

"Yes. I know it hurts you and that you're missing Emma, but let us focus on Aaron. Not Emma or Steven or Alice or Xander. Let us just focus on Aaron, please."

"Okay. Yeah, okay, like we agreed. I'll stay clear of him, I won't bring anything up."

"Thank you, Dustin. Now, the bike?"

"It's just in my car. Something in the bag *really* stinks, though."

"Ugh, that'll be the pastry he put in there on Monday and kept forgetting about. It was already off by the middle of the week... when will that boy ever learn!"

Magda ushered Dustin out of the front door and begun to help Dustin get the bike out of the back of his car, both completely unaware that Aaron, wrapped in his duvet and still drenched with sweat, had been watching their exchange from the top of the stairs.

## Chapter Twenty-Four

It had been three days, and Dan was getting worried. Other than the perpetually late Connor, he hadn't had a student absence from 13DV all term. Then last week he got berated by both Aaron and the head-teacher, and now Aaron was absent. He was sure it was nothing to do with him, but he couldn't shake the feeling of guilt, and that something was wrong.

"Sir, it's almost break, should we save our work?"

He was pulled from his daydreaming by the small, quiet student in front of him. Whatever was up with Aaron Grayling, he still had a class to teach.

"Thank you, Josh" he said quietly to the student and then, much louder, "okay class, save and log off please!"

Just as the last student had turned off their screen, the bell sounded for break time. Dan bid his students farewell and closed the door behind them.

"Maybe I should just call and find out what's going on. I *am* his tutor, after all."

Strolling over to his cupboard with newfound purpose, he pulled out the file labelled with the name of his tutor group and started thumbing through the papers until he found the one for Aaron Grayling.

"Next of kin Magda Grayling, okay." He picked up his phone, tapped in the number, and hit dial.

Ring ring. Ring ring. Ring ring.

"Hello, Magda speaking."

"Oh… err… hi. I mean, hello. I'm Dan Varley, I'm Aaron's tutor."

"Hello, what can I do for you?

"I… Well. Aaron hasn't been at school this week so far, and I just wondered if everything was okay. I mean, I just…"

"Is this the same Mr Varley that I had to complain about last week for perpetually ignoring my son's request to talk to you about physics degrees?"

"Err... yes."

"And now you're so interested my son's life that you're calling me in the middle of the day to see whether or not he is feeling any better?

"I just...he's been absent and... we have a policy where..."

"I know all about your policy. Are you aware of my son's health issues?"

"I... Sort of."

"Sort of. Well, Mr Varley, you should know that your policy is being followed. I let George Croft know that Aaron wouldn't be in this week. But the reasons for that are between him and this family, not the subject of tutor wonderings or staff room gossip."

"I didn't mean... I wouldn't..."

"Tell me then, Mr Varley, why are you only now suddenly concerned for my son?"

"I just... was worried? He hadn't been absent at all for the rest of the term and I just thought... maybe something…"

"Maybe you suddenly feel bad… ganze schlecht behandelt!"

"What?"

"You treated him badly! You treated him differently because of your rumours and your gossip and now you think he might be off school because of it and you feel bad. It's called *guilt*, Varney, it does not take a physicist to work *that* out."

"I… err… I'm sorry."

"Don't be. Aaron is just sick. He had the flu and will be back at school next week."

"Okay… is there… anything I can…"

"He will be back at school next week. Now goodbye, Varney."

"G… good…"

The call ended, the speaker on his phone falling silent. Dan placed it back down on his desk and stared at it incredulously, as if he couldn't quite believe what had just transpired. He *knew* that he had been treating Aaron differently because of the rumours about his health, but he hadn't realised anyone else had noticed. Then George came to see him last week, and now the dressing-down he just got from his mother...

He deserved it, he thought. He'd broken one of the fundamental rules of teaching, and one of his own ethical rules too. Always bullied as the tiny kid at secondary school, he swore when he got into teaching that he would never stand by and let another student be treated the way he was. And now what? Not only was he standing idly by, he was *causing* the problem.

His face burned hotly with shame. How could he undo the damage? Suddenly he remembered— Aaron had left his school planner last week, and Dan had put it in his desk drawer ready to return it to him on Monday morning. Perhaps he'd made some notes on what universities he was looking at, so he could do a bit of research and get back into Aaron (and his mother's) good books when he got back to school next week.

Pulling out the thick, wire-bound planner, he placed it down on the desk and opened the first page. It had Aaron's name and tutor group, and his timetable. Nothing out of the ordinary there, he thought, and he began to flick through the pages of the term that they were fast approaching the end of. Homework notes, more homework notes, his UCAS login details… wait. Dan stopped at the page from a few weeks ago and did a double take.

"Who killed Emma?" he said aloud to himself as he read the short note hastily scrawled in the footer of the page. "Emma who?"

He flicked ahead to the next week and found equally confusing scrawling around the page. Phrases like 'Dustin is prime suspect' and 'Murder in Meriville' were all over it, and seemed to continue as he came closer to the present. He turned to the current week's page in the planner, which was blank except for one sentence in the note's column for Friday.

'Call the police if no progress is made on murder investigation.'

Dan sat and looked at the planner, unsure what to think. On the one hand, none of these notes seemed to make any sense—but on the other hand, they were *just* worrying enough for him to feel like he needed to take action. But what should he do? If he talked to the headteacher he'd probably end up getting in trouble, and he didn't particularly want to call Aaron's mother again.

Pulling open his laptop, he opened up a browser window and did a search for 'Meriville police non emergency number.' Tapping the number for the local police station's main reception into his phone, he hit call and thought about what he was going to say. After three rings, the call connected.

"Hello, Meriville Constabulary, how can I help?"

"I, err, hello. I'm not sure really. I just found some random scribbling in one of my students notebooks and I guess I wanted to ask… are there, err, any murders currently being investigated in this town?"

"Let me put you through to youth services."

The phone started ringing again, and Dan started to breath a little heavier. Was he mad?

"Youth services, how can I help?"

"Oh hi, err, I'm a teacher at the local academy and one of my students has written something in their planner about a murder, and I just wanted to check if…"

"Aaron Grayling?"

"Err… yes, how did you…"

"For goodness sake, stay out of it and stop wasting our time. Goodbye."

The line went dead and Dan put his phone back

down on the desk after receiving his second vocal telling off of the day and tried to make sense of what had just happened. Stay out of it? Stay out of *what?*

Murder in Meriville? Perhaps there's some method in Aaron's madness after all.

## Chapter Twenty-Five

There was a crack in the ceiling. It wasn't a huge one, but it was definitely new. Aaron lay in bed squinting at it, trying to gauge how long it was. Half a metre, maybe? It'd probably be twice that size in a few months, he thought. This house really did need some work, and every time there was a big storm the inevitable decay only seemed to happen faster and faster.

He yawned, stretched, and rolled over. He'd been feeling low on energy since that fateful Monday, and four days in bed didn't seem to have made him feel much better. That said, his brain was still jumbled over it all. He remembered being in the woods, and he remembered with a shiver the gut-wrenching agony on discovering the hut had been destroyed... but then he woke up in his bed, with his Mum trying to force-feed him tea. He had no idea how he got home, or what happened after he collapsed in the rubble.

And then there was Dustin, here again visiting his Mum and returning his bike from the woods, and talking about people he'd never heard of before. Xander... was that X? And Emma, it must be the same one.Why was his mum telling Dustin to forget about her?

"None of this makes any sense"

"What doesn't, Kleine?"

He'd been so lost in his own world that he hadn't heard his mother come up the stairs.

"Oh, nothing Mum. What's up?"

"I made you another tea. I've got to go shopping, will you be okay for a couple of hours?"

"Mum, I'm just sick, I'll be fine."

"Okay, call me if you need me though okay? Is your phone charged?"

He'd barely given his phone a thought. Nobody ever

called or texted, but he hadn't even considered that it had been in his pocket when he fell.

"Oh yes, here it is on the side."

Magda unplugged it and put it on top of Aaron's duvet.

"You know where I am if you need me. And dinner tonight is käse spätzle, your favourite!"

"Thanks, Mama."

Magda left the room and Aaron picked up his phone. No scratches. A miracle really, he thought, given as he was writhing around in rubble. Not that he supposed it mattered now, with no hut and no journal. He placed his finger on the home button and unlocked the phone. There, on the screen before him, was the message that Dustin had left for him.

'Hey, It's Dustin. Found you next to the woods in a bad way. Brought you home and sorted you out without your Mum knowing anything. Don't tell her I helped. Just get better soon. BTW borrowed some trackies. Long story.'

He read it over and over, trying to make sense of it. He 'sorted me out'? Aaron suddenly realised that he had mysteriously gone from being fully clothed in his uniform to naked in bed, and recoiled in horror at the realisation that Dustin may now have been the one that put him there. He started breathing heavily. Dustin had to 'borrow' a pair of his tracksuit bottoms, too? What the hell had happened? What possible situation could have led to the two them being naked together?

He sat up in bed and let his body calm itself down. This was even more confusing than not knowing how he got home, and he hated it. The conspiracy that Dustin and his Mum seemed to have against him, Dustin putting him to bed and god knows what else. This wasn't just a murder investigation anymore—the people he knew were involved, and were keeping things from him.

He got out of bed and walked over to his desk. Sitting down, he pulled the fresh cup of tea that his mother had brought towards him and took a sip. It helped to revive a bit of his energy, and he looked back down at his phone. Opening up the pictures app, he started to look through the photos of what remained of the hut. He still wasn't sure what had happened to it, but whatever it was had happened in a big way. He was trying to jog his own memory, too. He knew that something had sent him over the edge, but he couldn't remember what in particular had triggered it. Everything was… foggy.

The images in his camera roll ended with a wide shot of the whole area. His eyes were drawn to something underneath one of the trees, and suddenly it was like a floodgate opened in his mind. The bricks, the message, the pain. He dropped his phone and ran back over to his bed, wrapping himself up in his duvet.

'Keep Looking Aaron'

Keep looking for what? Was the journal still out there? Had X just moved it to another hut, deeper in the woods? Or perhaps the message meant that he should keep looking for the killer. Either way, Aaron thought, he was sick of getting messages passed to him while nobody actually talked to him directly.

Getting out of bed resolutely, he picked his phone back up and deleted the photo. It wasn't going to scare him any longer. He rummaged around in his drawer for a clean pair of tracksuit bottoms and a t-shirt, threw them on, and headed out of his room and down the stairs.

Magda was always one for cleanliness, but Aaron was convinced she must have been stress-cleaning while he'd been confined to his room. The downstairs of the house was *spotless*, to the degree that Aaron felt bad for so much as thinking about treading on the carpet. He walked into the living room and immediately found his target.

His Mum's laptop sat in its usual position on the side table by the window. It never moved, leading Aaron to comment to her many times that she ought to have just bought a desktop computer. She also had a bad habit of leaving it logged in, which would definitely serve to Aaron's advantage today. Sitting down in the chair in front of the screen, he clicked the mouse and watched as the screen came to life.

"Yes!" he exclaimed aloud. She had left the computer logged in.

"Alright, where do you keep all of your contacts."

He clicked through a few of the open applications, and found her email logged in. Clicking through to 'people' he clicked search box at the top of the page, typed 'Dustin' and pressed find. While he and Dustin had a few mutual friends on Facebook, his messages were closed and he couldn't send him a friend request. This was the only way he could think of finding a way to contact him… and there it was, Dustin's mobile number. Pulling his phone from his pocket he quickly transcribed the number from the screen of his mother's laptop into a new contact, hit save, and returned the screen on the laptop to the email inbox that was on there before. He looked back to his phone and opened up messages.

'To: Dustin


Hey. It's Aaron. And I need answers.'


Send.

## Chapter Twenty-Six

"Okay, so I've gone through all of your UCAS forms and made comments on your personal statements and highlighted anything that might get flagged up in the system and potentially hold up your applications, so take these back and work on the feedback over Christmas. Those of you working on apprentice applications, I've done the same with your personal statements. The rest of you have your individual feedback sheets to be working on, so there's plenty for you all to think about during the break."

The bell rung, accompanied shortly after by the sound of chairs scraping on the old linoleum flooring. Dan Varley's tutor group were ready to move on to their first class of the day.

"Don't forget to collect your sheets on the way out! Oh, and Grayling? You left your planner here last week so please grab that on your way our. And, err, could you, um, come back and see me at break time please to chat Physics? Thank you, everyone. Have a great day."

Aaron shuffled out of the room, slightly red-faced from having been called out in front of the class, but even more confused as to his tutor's intentions. He'd spent the entire term so far avoiding Aaron like the plague, and now suddenly he wanted to chat? Aaron couldn't shake the feeling that it was something ominous.

"Varley likes Aaron!" came a shout from across the corridor. It was Connor, the perpetually late idiot, and his partner in crime Joe.

"Yeah, what is it, like a date at break or something?"

"Grow up, you two." Aaron replied wearily—from their first day at school together, the pair had goaded him.

"Better than growing outwards. For Mr. Varley."

"I don't even... you two are so lame."

"Whatever, loverboy."

The pair turned down a corridor heading away from Aaron, and he breathed a sigh of relief. Their incessant teasing didn't really bother him that much, but it did add to his unease at having to return to see his tutor during morning break. It was going to be a long ninety minutes until then.

He opened the door to the library and shuffled in, deep in thought. The place was empty again, save for the librarian. He was sure that there'd be a few lower school kids coming and going during the next two periods, but they rarely came over to the study area that Aaron ensconced himself in regularly. He pulled out his physics books and opened them with a sigh. It wasn't that he was falling out of love with the subject that was so close to his heart, but he found himself more and more distracted as days went by. He really did want answers—from his mother, from Dustin, and from the now absent X— but nobody would shed any light on anything.

He'd tried hunting for the journal again, too, figuring that's what the words under the tree meant. As soon as he'd felt well enough after… whatever it was that happened when he found the hut the way it was, he went out on his bike and searched the woods the best he could. There were still bits he hadn't managed to reach, but with builders now swarming the place it was hard to search undetected.

Aaron leaned back in the chair and yawned. He was *exhausted* for whatever reason, and it had just hit him like a baseball bat. He picked up one of the books and tried to focus on it, forcing his eyes down the page but not really taking in anything that he was reading. His eyes were responding sluggishly, and his arms felt heavy. A fuzzy, warm blanket seemed to be creeping over his consciousness and the book he was reading fell to his side as his head lolled back and he drifted off to sleep.

\* \* \*

Again the fog surrounded him, transporting him from wherever he was in the real world to this world of surreality and nightmare. He was sitting on the smooth, solid bench from his first few dreams, but the fog around him was so think he couldn't tell what else might be around him. If it wasn't for the fact that he felt the bench beneath him, he'd think he was flying.

He knew the drill by now. If he got up and ran, he'd just keep running until he got tired. If he stayed still, things would eventually swoop down at him from the fog and scream their tortured screams. It was getting... old.

"I'm sick of this!" Aaron screamed into the fog. "Sick of your mystery. Sick of being the one to never find anything out. Sick of this stupid fog."

He'd have continued his complaint but he suddenly detected a faint rumbling through his feet. A tremor, very slight, surging through the floor and up through his cold, bare soles. Suddenly, something flashed in his vision up ahead. A red spark, arching across the fog. Aaron felt a flash of heat. It was fire, the fog was turning to fire before his eyes.

The heat was intense but he seemed somehow protected from it, like the field of flames parted around him and met again past his back. He reached his arm out in curiosity, and found that no matter how hard he tried, he couldn't touch the maelstrom of fire. The place looked oddly familiar now, too—the fire was casting silhouettes of old buildings and benches, he was sure he'd been here before.

"Well, I said I was sick of the fog, so I guess you

heard me…"

"Aaron" came a voice through the flames. It seemed familiar, and yet, he couldn't place it. It sounded wounded, somehow in pain.

"Who are you? How do you know me?"

"It's me." Came the mysterious reply. It could be anyone, and yet, somehow Aaron knew. He was finally making contact.

"X? Is that you?"

"Yes. Have you found the journal yet?"

"No, I've been trying but I just can't seem to work out where it is."

"I'll get it to you. We don't have much time left."

"What do you mean?"

"I… I think I'm…"

Suddenly noise surrounded him like a bustling sort of buzzing sound, and Aaron was having trouble making out what X was saying.

"You're what? I can't hear you."

"Dying."

Aaron awoke with a start, sitting up suddenly in his

chair and sending his physics book flying across the room. Several first-year students were stood nearby and giggled at the sudden re-awakening of the strange sixth-former they often saw sat in the library.

"I… err…"

"The bell just went for break" said one of the first years, slightly apologetically.

"Thanks."

Running his hands over his face, he found himself unable to shake what had just happened. "It was just a dream" he said to himself, as he tried to get his thoughts in order.

"Break time! Crap! I've got to go see Varley."

\* \* \*

"Come in, Aaron."

"Thanks, sir."

"Are you okay? You look kind of, well, exhausted to be honest."

"I'm fine, sir. Just not slept well the past few nights,

that's all."

Aaron sat down in a chair facing Dan Varley's desk. His form tutor always looked a little nervous, but seemed to be twitching and stuttering more than usual. He was really perplexed by the man—he was a teacher, and yet seemed somehow less mature than half of the students. Not because of his height or anything, but the fact that he'd been avoiding Aaron for the past term had really irritated him. He'd have to push back on it, he thought.

"Oh, sorry to hear that. Well, err, first off, so, you want to go on and study physics at university, and I know you wanted to chat about…"

"Yes, " interrupted Aaron. "At the start of term. Weeks ago, months even. And you've been totally avoiding me. No offence, sir, but I'm kind of unsure why you've suddenly decided I'm worth the time of day when it seemed like the last thing you wanted to give me when I first asked."

"Ah, err, umm, well, I, err"

"You've already said all of that. Less of the stalling, more of the explaining please. I *do* want to talk physics, but how do you expect me to respect you when you can't look me in the eye?!"

Aaron was breathing deeply. In his entire life, he had never talked to a teacher in that way before, and he really struggled with standing up to authority figures like this. But damn it, this teacher was treating him like crap, and he was only being honest. Looking up, he realized that Mr. Varley had tears in his eyes and in an instant he went from feeling anger to feeling remorse.

"Oh, sir, I didn't mean to…"

"No, no, it's okay. You're right, I've been really awful. And I'm sorry. I just… I just don't know how to handle everything. I've only been a teacher for a year and a term and I'm… God, students aren't meant to see me like this!"

"Mr. Varley. I.. I won't tell anyone, it's fine. It wasn't my intention to make you cry, I just wanted answers."

"I *have* been unfair, and I'm sorry. I was terrified of talking to you, but it's obvious that I shouldn't have been. I'm just so sorry."

"Do you want me to come back later?"

"No, let's finally have that physics talk."

Dan wiped his eyes and tried to steady his breathing.

"So what area of physics interests you the most?"

"Well, I love the theoretical side of things, but it's space that really fascinates me. I've always loved the idea that there are worlds beyond our own. I'm a sci-if fan for that reason, not that it makes me the most popular. I mean, I was the nerdy kid that started year seven with a Star Trek backpack and it took years to live that down."

"Ha, you and I are far more similar than I thought."

"Oh, really? Who's your favorite captain then, sir?"

"Picard, but Janeway's a close second. Everyone's all 'Kirk this and Sisko that' but sometimes…"

"Sometimes you've just got to punch your way through!"

The pair laughed, and it felt to Aaron that his tutor probably didn't get to laugh a lot at school. The anger that he was feeling was very quickly subsiding, and he felt a new wave of… not respect, but something more akin to understanding. He'd been the nerdy kid at school once, too.

"So are you thinking applied or theoretical for Astro?"

"To be honest, I'm not totally sure yet. I love the

practical stuff, getting hands on with telescopes and maybe even actual space hardware is pretty exciting to me, but then I do love the idea of contributing to the next big breakthrough in understanding the universe."

"Ah yes, well, obviously there's Oxford for Astrophysics, but Imperial and St Andrews are really hot on Oxford's tail these days. I went to Manchester and it was excellent, but I was always a little sad that I didn't choose Imperial."

"You weren't tempted by Oxford?"

"Tempted, yes, but I didn't really want to subject myself to the lifestyle that comes with being a student at Oxford University, if you get my meaning."

"Yes, I have similar feelings."

"St. Andrews is lovely but it is just so remote. There isn't much traditional student nightlife there."

"That would suit me to be honest, as long as there's somewhere I can cycle I'm happy."

The bell signaling the end of break sounded loudly in the classroom, surprising both Aaron and his form tutor.

"Oh, I hadn't realized the time, sorry Aaron but I've got a year seven class coming in next, otherwise I'd be happy to continue chatting."

"No worries, sir, I've got to head off to a lesson now anyway. But… thanks. It's actually been really nice talking."

"Yes, um, it kind of has hasn't it? And thanks, you know, for the discretion around my…"

"I don't know what you mean, sir. Nothing happened."

Aaron winked as he left the classroom, realising that he had just treated his form tutor more as a friend than a teacher. Oh well, he thought, no harm done. He actually seemed nice.

## Chapter Twenty-Seven

The days were at their shortest, and Aaron hated the cycle home from school at this time of year. It was bitingly cold, yet unforgivingly sweaty once he started cycling. The woodland through which he cycled had started to change, too. Diggers and other equipment had moved in, and a giant sign had been erected at the edge that faced the town informing all who cared to glance in its direction that a new housing estate was soon to appear there.

He stopped, as he often did, at the remains of the hut.

Most of the area had been cleared now, but the

concrete base and some of the splinters of wood from the felled roof were still strewn around the area. The fence panel had been replaced and, he noted with amusement, secured into place with cable ties and a few more metal clips than before.

He poked his fingers through the metal fencing and grasped it, looking down at the devastation, deep in thought about his dream in the library. X had said he'd send him the journal, but he wasn't convinced. It was a dream, all in his own head. And yet, the night before he went and found the hut destroyed, he'd dreamed he was laying in mud with crashing sounds all around him. Was it some kind of prophecy?

He shook his head and, with one last look back over the ruinous scene in front of him, he put his feet back on the pedals and started back on the journey towards home.

Cycling through the clearing, Aaron was pleased to see the lights on at home. It looked like his mother was on her laptop in the living room, so he should be able to slip in, say a quick hello, and head up to his room to relax a little. The lights in the kitchen and conservatory weren't on, and as he continued on the path to the rear of the house his bike light was once again the only source of illumination nearby.

His mind focused on getting home, he almost didn't notice when his bike light picked up something reflective by the back door into the conservatory. What was that? It was small, almost like a phone book or box of charity bin bags propped against the door, but he knew that those things would be delivered to the front. He was the only one who used the back door.

Ten feet away, the object started to come into focus, and his blood froze. He knew exactly what it was— the journal that X had promised him.

How was this even possible? Aaron felt a cold wave of terror rush over him. Not only were his dreams coming true, but X knew where he lived. He'd always felt safe in his house, like it could be a world away from the journal if he needed it to be. And yet here, in a clear plastic bag and propped expectantly up against the back door, the book stood.

Aaron looked behind him fearfully, expecting someone to jump out from the shadows. Nobody did, though. It was just him, the journal, and the darkened conservatory. He fumbled for his keys, opened the door, and quickly pulled his bike and the journal in from the cold.

"Is that you, dear?"

His mother called from the kitchen. As it if could be anyone else.

"Yes, Mama, hello."

"Good day?"

"Err, yeah, just want to go up and get changed."

Picking up the journal and his school bag, he quickly moved through the dark kitchen and headed straight up the stairs to his bedroom. He closed the door behind him with a thud, threw his bag down, and put the journal on his desk. He sat down in his desk chair and just stared at it, as if he could somehow will it to disappear.

The journal itself looked to be in worse condition than when Aaron had last seen it. Through the plastic bag it was in he could see that there were more scratches, and that the spine had taken a bit of a beating. There was more mud, too. It had clearly not found a place as stable nor as well protected as the hut it had previously called home.

Opening the bag carefully, Aaron slid the journal out and placed it back down on the desk. He had almost got used to the idea that he'd never see it again, and now here it was delivered to him by people or forces unknown. It had somehow taken on a more mystical quality than it had previously.

Slowly, almost cautiously he picked up the journal, slid off the elastic, and opened it. Flicking through the damper-than-usual pages, he found the most recent entries and started to read.

'I am making progress with Dustin. I think he knows far more than he is letting on, and I hope that you have also had some success with him Aaron. There is something very odd about his involvement in this situation. How have your investigations gone at school? Have you thought about talking to people in your family about when and where they last saw Emma? I look forward to hearing more.'

Turning the page, the writing was much less neat and the page was covered in dirt.

'My hut, my sanctuary, has been destroyed. How could they. How could they even know about it? They are trying to stop me getting to the truth, I know it. I was able to retrieve the journal from the wreckage but why destroy the only place I truly feel at home? Was it the police? Did they decide to finally shut down my investigation? Or maybe the killer discovered my trail and wanted to intimidate me. Either way, Aaron, help me. I hope you find this.'

There was more, several pages of similar rhetoric continued.

'I can only assume you have been unable to find the journal yet. Either that or they got to you, too. I had a dream about you the other night, you were at the old ticket office of the abandoned train station in the woods. At least, I think it was you. It was very foggy, and I don't know what you look like but I just knew it was Aaron. Why are you in my dreams? I have nowhere to go now, no other huts or buildings. I write this in the mud and dirt.'

The final entry in the journal made even less sense.

'I do not know how, but they've got me. They have poisoned me, I think. I'm certain that I'm dying. I feel myself getting weaker every day. My mind is going, I think. I cannot even process simple things any more. If I die, Aaron, please find justice. For me. For Emma. For us all. Please help us.'

Aaron put the journal down and looked at the pages in disbelief. The fog dreams, X thinking that they are dying… it was all stuff he'd dreamed too. How was that possible? Was there some deeper connection between him and X that he had somehow overlooked? His eyes flicked back to the last entry and a lightbulb went off in his mind. The old station ticket office! That's where his dreams had been based. He knew it had seemed familiar, but he just hadn't been able to connect the bench and the fog with a real location.

As he'd read the entries, he was very willing to shrug most of X'S rantings as nothing more than conspiracy theory and madness—but the mention of that dream and a location only a 10 minute cycle into the woods really made Aaron wonder whether this really was nonsense, or whether there was some fundamental, deeper meaning to it all.

Suddenly, he had a thought. Dustin still hadn't replied to his text message, but what if there was a way that Aaron could corner him into feeling compelled to respond? After all, X was naming him as the suspect in both Emma and his own potential deaths.

He pulled out his phone, opened up the as-yet-one-sided text message conversation with Dustin, and began typing.

'Dustin, be honest now. Did you kill Emma?"

He hit send, and put his phone down on the desk next to the journal. Standing up, he walked over to the mirror and began to strip, finally shucking the dankly-smelling school clothes he'd been in all day. He was just about done when suddenly, unexpectedly, he heard his text message alert noise. Rushing over to the desk mostly-naked, he looked down and saw that he'd received a text message from Dustin. Finally. He opened it up and read the six-word response with more questions than answers.

'You're not supposed to know Emma'

## Chapter Twenty-Eight

Magda called up the stairs to Aaron again, irritation in her voice.

"Come on, Kleine, dinner is ready. I don't want to have to call you again!"

She shuffled back into the kitchen and lowered her tone.

"Remember that he is a teenager, and almost an adult, he's probably busy doing what all boys do at that age."

She busied herself with the kettle, making some ginger tea to have with her food. It wasn't the best combination, but she'd once heard that it helped with digestion and she'd felt compelled to make use of that fact ever since.

Aaron had seemed to recover fairly quickly from the flu he had picked up. Once his fever had subsided he seemed to be back to his normal self. Yet the past few days he'd seemed distracted again, like something was weighing heavily on his mind. She hoped he'd been taking his medication—it was his responsibility to manage it as a 17 year old, but she knew it was hard. The doctor had warned her of that when he'd listed off what seemed like a hundred side effects. Still, Aaron wanted them, and she was happy to be supporting him.

"Sorry, Mama, I was just getting changed."

Aaron bounded into the kitchen in his tracksuit bottoms and a t-shirt, phone in hand, looking a little red faced but largely seeming fine. He seemed glued to his phone screen, though, and as he sat down at the table ready to eat, he took the very unusual step of placing his phone right beside him, screen on, staring at it intently.

"It's fairly simple tonight, sorry about that. I didn't have much time to prepare anything complicated today."

"Mum, you don't need to be sorry for not cooking huge meals every night. Whatever it is, it'll be great."

"I thought I'd try out this recipe for stuffed marrow…"

"Unless it's stuffed marrow, which you know I hate."

"Just kidding, Kleine, did you break your funny bone on the way home? It's just some chicken and pasta."

"Sounds great. "

Aaron continued to keep an eye on his phone as Magda got out two plates and began to serve up the food she'd prepared for her and her son. He usually groaned and grimaced at her attempts to humorously lie to him, but it had totally passed him by tonight. Maybe he *is* really distracted about something. Was it his phone, perhaps? She waddled over with a couple of plates and set them down on the table in the usual spots.

"So what's so important on that phone screen of yours?

"Huh?"

"You never normally use your phone that much,

and here you are staring at it like it's some long lost love. Ah! Is it some new special person in your life?"

"No Mum, I'm just waiting for a friend to text me back about something, that's all. Although speaking of new people in my life, my form tutor Mr. Varley finally found some time to talk to me about physics today."

"Oh really? What did he have to say?"

"Well, we share the same favorite Star Trek captain."

"That's not exactly physics…"

"No, but we did talk universities too, and the best ones for astrophysics. He confirmed that the ones I've put down as my choices are right, and we talked a little about different areas and specialisms."

"That sounds really good. Did he apologise for not having helped you before now?"

"He did actually, yeah. He seems like a pretty nice guy for a teacher."

"Well dear, I'm glad. Although is he sure about St. Andrews?"

"Yeah, it's a great place for astrophysics, and I like the idea of going somewhere a little further from home."

"But it's so far away! And there's such little there! Do you really want to be in a place that's so cut off from the world?"

"I've always wanted to live somewhere less sleepy than Meriville, and the whole city is basically a proper student village without it being too overwhelming. And besides, imagine the chances for good cycling there'll be there!"

The pair continued eating in relative silence, with Aaron checking his phone screen almost constantly. She tried to catch a glimpse of what was on the screen, but couldn't make anything out at this distance. It was just a blur of pixels that looked like words, but which words they actually were was anyone's guess.

"I'm not used to having to compete with a phone screen for your love, you know."

Aaron looked up, and his face flushed red with annoyance. He loved his mother, but she had really hurt him by lying about Dustin, and maybe about Emma too. Without thinking, he snapped a response back at her.

"Well I'm not used to not being able to trust you,

Mama"

"What?"

"I'm...I'm sorry. I'm just still not sure about this whole Emma thing and..."

"I told you that she was someone from university, and..."

"You said childhood friend."

"It's the same thing. Enough now."

Aaron felt bad. He was being lied to, and her slip up on the details proved it, but he couldn't bring himself to hate her for too long. He sat silently frustrated, both at Magda and at himself for reacting so hotly. Finally, his mother broke the silence—and tension—by changing the subject.

"I'm glad you got to talk to Varley, anyway."

"Thanks, Mama. What did you do with your day?"

"I've been online all day talking to people about these damned new houses. They're going to completely destroy the woodland out there, and there was absolutely no public consultation first. There was the fence, then the sign, and then a flyer through the door. I mean, think of all the wildlife that's in there! Not to mention it's going to make enough noise to keep us irritated for however long it takes to build, and then there's the matter of access and increased footfall on the pa-"

Aaron's phone made a loud noise and the screen lit up with a new message, interrupting Magda and totally distracting Aaron from what she was saying. Aaron looked down at the screen with an intensity that she rarely say him exude, and he suddenly pushed back his chair and stood bolt upright.

"Sorry, Mama, I need to go and, I mean, I want to, and I, err, I need to reply to this in private."

"Go on, Kleine, go do what you need to do. I'll put the rest of this in the microwave for later."

Without a word of thanks, Aaron turned and ran upstairs. She heard the door to his room close loudly, and sighed.

"Oh, to be young" she said under her breath, as she continued to eat her dinner alone.

## Chapter Twenty-Nine

Dustin stared at the message from Aaron, not sure what to think. When he'd initially tried to make contact, it was easy to just ignore it as per his agreement with Magda—but now he'd mentioned Emma and he wasn't sure what to do.

Aaron had mentioned Emma to him once before, but he had only had a chance to express vague surprise that Aaron knew of her existence at all. This was a chance to find out how Aaron had got to know of her, and what it all meant. If nothing else, there were significantly more questions than answers right now.

Magda had assured him that Aaron didn't know Xander, or Emma, and yet here he was asking about her. Reading her name was like a wound opening, and he felt a swelling pain grow in his chest. Part of him wanted to throw the phone away and ignore it, but he knew he couldn't do that. He had to know.

'You're not supposed to know Emma.' He replied, instantly regretting it. There was no going back now, the floodgates had been opened.

'How does that matter? I asked you if you had killed someone.'

Aaron's reply was steeped in twisted logic. He didn't really know Emma, did he? He's just heard that someone called Emma has died, and now he's accusing him of the murder. But how had he made that connection? Dustin was confused and curious, as he sat and thought carefully about his next response.

Some minutes passed, and another message from Aaron popped up on his phone screen. Clearly he was sat at home stewing over this.

'So you aren't denying it?'

Dustin replied quickly, hurt by Aaron's accusations.

'Of course I am. Do you really think I'm capable of killing anyone?'

It wasn't the response he'd wanted to send, but the idea that anyone might think that he was a killer made Dustin shake with rage. He was a pacifist, always had been, and he couldn't ever harm anyone. In the twenty years he'd been alive, he'd only been in one fight, and that was enough to make him never want to do it again. Murder? He wasn't capable of it. Another response came in from Aaron.

'Love makes people do crazy things.'

'Yes, but I know myself. You should too. I am not a killer. Emma is gone, and I grieve for her.'

He had well and truly broken his promise to Magda, and was steadily tumbling down a rabbit hole that he feared he'd never be able to get himself out of. Her plan for a peaceful and clean transition was coming undone with each message the pair exchanged.

'As far as I know she's just missing. How do you know she is really dead? Why don't the police care?'

Dustin was wondering how he could have such intimate knowledge of a situation he was neither involved in nor meant to know anything about. Suddenly, though, it hit him. The last time he talked to Xander, he really pushed Dustin for information on who lived at the old farm house. With a sudden moment of hindsight, the realised he had mentioned Aaron's name. Had Xander and Aaron been talking? Was that even possible? Magda had assured him that it wasn't, but now he wasn't so sure

'We said our goodbyes. She's gone.'

He wasn't sure if he should be going into detail with Aaron, but the poor guy must feel like he's being lied to left, right, and centre. Dustin had always been firmly against this plan, and now that Aaron was contacting him directly he couldn't cope with lies and secrets any more.

'You knew she was going to die? And she knew she was going to die? Then this isn't a murder?'

How was he meant to explain this without the entire situation coming undone? He thought long and hard, and the only thing he could think to reply with was lamer than anything he'd ever want to receive himself.

'It's complicated.'

'Well make it uncomplicated. I am sat here accusing

you of murder and you can't even explain the situation? How do you think the police would react to this? Or the general public? I am so close to putting wanted posters up all over town with your face on, Dustin. So come clean. What the hell is going on?'

This was it, thought Dustin. From here, he could either ignore or engage, and there was no way that he could back out now. He didn't believe that Aaron would really put up posters everywhere, but at the same time he knew that he'd never quit, not until he'd found out the truth.

'Okay. I'll explain. But not over text. Meet me somewhere private next week?'

He couldn't face this today. He needed some time to prepare.

'Alone with you so that you can say goodbye to me like you did to Emma? I don't trust you.'

'I'm not explaining over text message, or the phone. It's in person or nothing.'

'Fine.'

'Okay. Meet me by the old ticket office in the woods on Monday night.'

Dustin was shaking. He'd bought himself the weekend to think about how best he was going to handle this. Aaron's text conversation fell silent, and Dustin's head hurt. Monday was going to be hell.

## Chapter Thirty

Aaron threw his leg over his bike and sat down hard into his saddle. It had been far too long since he'd put his cycle gear on, and ordinarily he'd be relishing the feeling. Today, though, he was far too angry to indulge in such pleasures.

He was meeting Dustin on Monday, which meant the entire weekend was going to be written off through stress. He'd woken up in a mood and decided that a heavy cycling session in the cold winter morning would be the best way to vent. At least, that was his hope. He *hated* feeling angry.

Pushing off, he did a speed lap around the house

before heading down the driveway and out onto the country roads that made up the outer part of Meriville.

The sky was clear and the sun was shining, but Aaron was still exceptionally cold all over. The warmth might come through later on, but for now he was cycling hard to try and keep from freezing.

Hitting a rhythm, he turned onto the road that ran between Meriville and Trenton. It was long—five and a half miles—and should provide him with ample opportunity to build up more speed and really thrash out his anger at higher speeds.

He was angry at Dustin. Fobbing him off for so long, ignoring his texts, and then replying with mystic nonsense? He couldn't work it out, he couldn't fathom it. What. Did. Any. Of. It. Mean.

He missed the turning he meant to take and continued on down the road. He had no real idea in his mind where he was going, but his idea to take the scenic route around the lakes had just become null and void. He kept going, letting the cold breeze wash over him, enjoying the refreshing freedom of Lycra as opposed to cycling in his school trousers and shirt during the week.

His anger started to subside, and he slowed down a

little. A new feeling filled his gut, and in many ways if felt worse than the blind rage he woke up with. The only way he could describe it was betrayal. Like all the people in his life seemed to want to keep him from the truth. None of them were on his side.

He felt a pang of loneliness. He'd always been fine spending time on his own, but suddenly he felt like there was nobody there he could lean on or trust. And it hurt.

He could see buildings up ahead, and he realised he was approaching Trenton. He rarely visited the place, but he vaguely remembered where things were. It was significantly larger than Meriville, and had a pretty huge college that he knew Dustin attended. There was a leisure centre too, which Aaron remembered going to as a child to learn to swim. That aside, the town was largely a mystery. Maybe it was finally time to go exploring.

Turning off the long road and onto the town's High Street, it was almost unrecognizable from the place he remembered as a child. A lot had changed in the past few years, including a massive pedestrianised area that seemed to replace must of the roadway around him.

"There must be a bike rack somewhere."

He saw some bikes parked up over by the fountain that marked the town centre, and headed toward it on foot. He hadn't thought to bring anything to throw over his cycle gear besides a hoodie, and he was drawing looks from people around. In this day and age, he couldn't believe that people gave two hoots about what someone else was wearing.

He fished around in his bike bag for his wallet, and locked the bag and the bike behind him. If he was going to be in town, he thought, then he might as well have some lunch or something. Besides, he found people watching quite stress relieving.

Walking along the newly-cobbled road, he spotted a half-empty cafe that seemed to serve panini and various other things. Coffee didn't really appeal to him, but the idea of tuna and melted cheese struck a chord and he headed inside.

It was like walking into an old-time western saloon. As the door swung closed behind him, everyone looked up from their plates and stared at him, clearly taken aback by a teenager in Lycra cycle gear walking into an establishment in which mostly elderly people were eating slowly as they wait for death to eventually consume them.

The morbidity of it all fascinated him, and he sat

down at one of the old-style wooden tables. There was a lot on the menu, but he knew what he wanted.

"Can I take your order please?"

The waitress that had come over couldn't have been much older than Aaron himself, and he was taken aback by that. In a sea of octogenarians, she was a shining jewel of youth. And damn, he thought, she was cute.

"Err, yeah, just a tuna melt panini please."

"Don't usually see people my age in here."

"Just halfway through a bike ride and wanted something to eat."

"Must keep you pretty fit."

"Well you must be pretty fit… I mean you should… Crap."

"Nice try mate, flirting not your strong point?"

"Not really. Sorry."

"I'll bring your panini over when it's ready."

The waitress smirked, clearly happy that she'd managed to cause Aaron a fair chunk of embarrassment, and walked off back behind the counter. It was nice to not be in Meriville, Aaron thought. At least here, nobody knows who he is and he doesn't know who any of these people were.

He smiled to himself. It had been a while since he'd flirted with a girl, and he was almost relieved to realize that he was still terrible at it. At least when he did meet one he could maybe think about dating, she'd have to be as awkward as he was.

His panini arrived and he ate in silence, looking out the window at the world going past. Parents and children, groups of people his own age. Why didn't he ever feel like he belonged with people like that? He'd always felt happier just being on his own.

Dustin returned to his thoughts, and he started to feel anxious. Monday was just 36 hours away now, and while a large part of him wished that it was just around the corner, a growing part of him felt a cold dread at what was to come.

Dustin's secrets were about to be revealed, and Aaron had a feeling that his world was about to change. Forever.

## Chapter Thirty-One

It was the last week of term, and Dan had given up thinking that the heating in his classroom would be fixed before the weather started getting warmer again. The maintenance team were apparently busy fighting fires—not literal ones—elsewhere in the school, but that didn't stop his need to wrap up in several layers just to enter his classroom early in the day. He knew the room would warm up once the heating flicked on, but he had the coldest room in the school and it was nothing short of unbearable in this weather.

Setting his bag down on the desk in front of him, he started busying himself for the day ahead. Last week of term activities were always a bit lighter. He'd be focusing on coursework with his older groups, but the younger ones could do some fun activities in the run up to Christmas. His favorite was to work out the forces involved in getting Santa's sleigh off the ground—a task that never failed to enthuse the first years. As he was getting out his planner, he heard the sound of a knock on his classroom door.

"Come in, it's unlocked!"

The door opened and Aaron Grayling walked through it. Easily the first student on the premises and earlier than anyone from his tutor group had ever been, Dan almost jumped in surprise to see him.

"Aaron! It's, err, it's really early. Everything okay?"

"Yeah, I just wanted to get in early and get some stuff done. Is that okay?"

"Certainly, go ahead and grab a computer or a desk or whatever you need."

Dan continued to prepare the mess of paperwork all over his desk as Aaron sat down in front of a computer and started working on whatever it is he was doing. It was still freezing cold, and he noticed that Aaron was shivering.

"Are you alright? I mean, are you really alright? You're shivering and you're here two hours before school starts. I shouldn't even let you be in here this early, or alone with me, but I can't exactly throw you out with it being even colder out there than it is in here."

"Yeah, I'm fine… Cold, I guess."

"Here, I've got a blanket in the cupboard, let me throw it over to you.

He'd brought this in to use on cold days when he was sitting doing not much else at his desk, but hadn't felt the need to use it yet this morning. Throwing it over, Aaron caught it and wrapped it around his slight, skinny frame.

"Thanks, sir. I appreciate it."

"If you want to talk about anything…"

"We only just got to talking about physics, sir. I think my life story would freak you out, or make you stutter nervously again."

"I, err, umm, err… I did read some interesting things in your planner…"

"You read my planner?"

"I… err…"

"Just notes from an English assignment. That's all."

The pair sat in silence for what felt like an eternity, and Dan tried his best to avoid making noise or generally drawing attention to his presence. On Friday he'd felt like a weight had been lifted, and that he'd finally managed to make a connection with Aaron after his failings this term, but this morning it felt like all of that progress had been lost. He was so inside his own head on this thinking that he almost missed Aaron speaking up again.

"Have you ever had… weird dreams?"

"Hmm? Well, I think everyone has the odd strange dream from ti-"

"No," Aaron pressed, "I mean *you.*"

"Well, yes, of course. Dreams are very personal, and don't always have a bearing on real life, though."

"Have your dreams ever predicted anything?"

"Like, could I somehow see Brexit happening in my dreams? No. I don't think they work like that."

"But I've had dreams over the past few months that really have. To be honest, that's what the notes in my planner were about. They've not directly predicted the future or anything, and it's not like

I've seen any images, but I've definitely had dreams where a voice has told me a thing would happen, and then it did."

"I, umm, I don't know what to say to that to be honest with you. Maybe you should talk to a counsellor or…"

"I'm just having weird dreams, that's all. Well, that's not all, but… oh, never mind."

"No, it's okay Aaron, you go ahead."

"I think I'm caught up in something, but I don't know what it is and it's freaking me out. I could barely sleep last night knowing I've got this meeting later, and I'm genuinely scared for my life."

"Caught up in… what? Like some sort of gang or-"

"No, no gang. Just with a person… people… who are hiding things from me. But I've been finding stuff out, and I want answers."

"I'm confused. What are these people doing to you? Are you in some kind of danger?"

"I don't know, sir. I think-"

There was a knock on the door, and the pair both jumped in their seats.

"Hello? Dan, are you in? I just wanted to catch up on… ah! Mr. Grayling, good to see you."

Dan watched as George Croft bounded through the door, his usual swagger seeming even more intense when crossed with festive joviality.

"Thanks, sir" Aaron replied, looking somewhat uncomfortable at having been interrupted mid-flow.

"What were the two of you brainboxes talking about then, eh?"

The pair paused.

"Err, umm, well-"

"Physics" Aaron replied, quickly cutting off the shuddering of his form tutor. "We were talking about the different approaches to theoretical astrophysics at different universities. You see, the professor at Oxford thinks that the Doppler shift we see in the universe is-"

"Woah, woah, woah" George interrupted, "you lost me at Oxford. All good with the mentoring then, Dan?"

"Yes, err, just love debating physics in the morning."

"Glad to hear it! I didn't mean to interrupt, Dan, I just wanted to see if you'd be up for running your

Santa's Sleigh activity at an assembly. I'll email you about it, let's catch up later."

"Okay, thanks George."

"Crofty!"

"Err…"

"See you later, gents!" George walked backwards through the door as he said his parting words. "Keep debating that physics!".

Dan looked at Aaron, who smiled shyly back at him.

"Thanks for covering for me, sir."

"Thanks for not dropping me in it!"

"How can you stand working for someone who thinks they're cool but are in fact the opposite?"

Dan laughed out loud, and the tension was once again broken.

"Okay, so where were we. You're in some kind of bad situation, you think? What can I do to help?"

"Well, I have an idea…"

## Chapter Thirty-Two

Aaron found his way through the fencing and headed into the part of the woods that would soon become houses. The old ticket office was far smaller than its name suggested, and Aaron had only really managed to find it successfully a couple of times before now.

He pushed on regardless, knowing that if he didn't get there then he'd likely never know the truth. He had provisions in place, and he was ready. Tonight he'd get the truth out of Dustin, whether he wanted to give it or not.

Walking through the cold woods, he was glad he'd

been able to go home and get changed before heading out. Besides, he didn't want to have to take his bike through this dense woodland, and the hole in the metal fence wasn't big enough to have got it through anyway. The last thing he wanted was a parked bike drawing attention to where he might be.

He continued on through the dark woods, trying his hardest to find some kind of torchlight or anything that might signal that Dustin was there waiting for him. Stumbling on, he saw what looked like a lantern up ahead and turned himself towards it. There was mist in the air, making everything seem damp.

Finally, up ahead, he saw a figure sat on a bench outside a very ruined small building. There was an LED lantern next to him kicking out a fairly large quantity of light which made the mist glow and almost look like fog.

"Aaron, is that you' the figure called out. The voice was familiar. Dustin was here.

"Yeah. Dustin?"

"The one and only."

"You can't just vanish me away, if you were thinking about doing that. I'd be missed."

"For the last time, man, I'm not a killer and I'm not going to lay a finger on you."

"Well forgive me for not trusting you."

"I do. I wouldn't trust me either in this situation."

Aaron sat down on the creaking wooden bench, the lantern the only thing between him and Dustin. He looked out into the distance, It was hard to believe that this area was once a bustling local train station. The Victorians really did know how to build a town.

"It's beautiful here, in a morbid kind of way" he said, almost forgetting his frustration and anger toward Dustin.

"Yeah, this was Emma's favourite spot. That's why I picked this place, actually. I thought that if I was finally going to honour both her memory and your curiosity with the truth, then this would be the most fitting place to do it."

"You really loved her, didn't you?"

"It's… complicated."

"Does it always get so misty here?"

"We're close to the lakes over at this end of the woods, it quite often gets foggy here at night. That's why I brought the lantern, it makes the whole area seem like it's lit up and alive when the fog rolls in."

"Okay, Dustin. Enough small talk. Tell me everything."

"Before I start, please know that I wanted you to know everything from the start. I was sworn to secrecy, though. It was meant to protect you, but…"

"Tell me *everything.*"

"okay. Well first off, nobody is dead."

"What? You said your goodbyes and she's not coming back, how could you not-"

"She's not really alive either."

"You're not making sense, Dustin. I'm warning you, if you don't sta-"

"Look, if you want the truth, stop interrupting me. This isn't going to be easy to tell and it's *definitely* not going to be easy to hear."

"Okay, go on."

"How much do you know about how the brain works?"

"What the… I guess a little, not loads, I'm a physicist not a biologist. But wha-"

"Have you ever heard the theory that the inside of our minds are infinite, and there can be a number of undiscovered worlds and realms on the *inside* of our heads, as well as there being undiscovered places and planets in the infinite universe *outside* of our heads?"

"What do you mean?"

"Some people, kind of like superheroes, can explore those worlds inside their minds better than others. They can channel different minds and different realities through the window of their mind. Emma was one of those people."

"You expect me to believe that Emma was some kind of superhero?"

"That's how I saw her. She wasn't alone, either. I knew a few of them, all here in Meriville. Steven, Alice, and Xander."

"Wait, is that Zander with a Z or Xander with an X?"

"With an X, why?"

"Oh my god, that's X."

"You… you know Xander? That's how he always used to sign his name."

"Used to? What happened to him?"

"Let me finish. I met Emma first out of all of them, and we fell in love. We'd been together for quite a while, really. It was very confusing at first—I didn't always know who I'd get to meet and when."

"What do you mean?"

"Well, they were all the same person. The same superhero. One window through which multiple people could live and experience the world, but not at the same time. Only one of them could look through the window at once. And they couldn't meet each other as a result."

"I'm not sure I follow you."

"The ignorant of the world call it Dissociative Identity Disorder, or DID. But those are the people who'd rather treat anything as a disorder or an illness than embrace it and allow someone to flourish as the person or people they really are."

"Dissociative… what?"

"Multiple personalities, dude."

"So wait, Emma and X are the same person?"

"They're two different people looking through one window."

"That's… a pretty liberal way of thinking about it. Sounds like a disorder to me."

"Anyway, it's totally different for different people. Some personalities in a plural system-"

"A what?"

"Seriously man, just trust me, there's a whole world of terminology out there and it's important to respect that. A plural system, a collection of these personalities that look through that window I keep mentioning."

"Right."

"Sometimes they are aware of each other's existence, and sometimes they aren't. It works totally differently for everyone, but the law doesn't really support or recognise that."

"So legally, Emma was the real person and X was some kind of… fake?"

"Not quite. Both Emma and Xander, along with the other people that I mentioned, were all part of a plural system, all different people able to look through that one window."

"The *window?* That's the real, physical person in all of this?"

"No, the window is a part of the system. But legally, the window is all that matters. The window gets to make the decisions. For example, if the window got a tattoo, everyone wakes up and realises they have one, whether they know where it came from or not."

"So what happened to everyone?"

"Well, like I said, the window is the one that gets to call the shots, whether they know it or not. And the window got offered an opportunity to lead a more… conventional life."

"Like a cure?"

"Well, there's always new medication on the market. In this instance, the doctors offered a solution that would kind of… suppress the system. They'd close the window and pull the blinds over it, meaning that…"

"… that the window would be the only thing the world would see. I think I get it, yeah."

Aaron paused, trying to take it all in. Emma and X were the same person, and they were both being killed by this drug.

"Wait a minute.' He said, a sudden realisation washing over him. "That means that there is a killer, or any least a suppressor. It's the window. The window killed Emma, killed X, killed all those other personalities."

"Remember man, nobody's really dead, they're just… gone."

"Jesus Dustin, how can you say that. It's as good as killing someone! It's criminal, that's what it is. How could you stand by while-"

"You think I had a choice?

Both Aaron and Dustin had got to their feet and were now yelling at one another, anger in both of their voices.

"You think I really wanted this to happen? I lost the love of my life, and some friends, all because the world was too cowardly to deal with people who are a bit different?"

"I'm… I'm sorry, Dustin."

"It's okay. I knew this was going to be hard. But I thought you had a right to know."

The pair sat back down, and Aaron saw Dustin wipe tears from his eyes. He stared out into the fog, now coming in thicker, making the area around them white with the combination of the lantern and the low cloud.

Several moments went past, and a question formed in Aaron's mind. One that terrified him, and one he wasn't sure he wanted to know the answer to. But the fog, the story... suddenly made sense. He felt dizzy, almost sick, as he drew the courage to ask the question.

"Dustin?"

"Yeah?"

"Who's the one that's left? Who's the window?"

Moments of silence followed.

"The *window*, Dustin. Who is it?

"Aaron, it's... You're the window."

Aaron got to his feet, the world around him spinning.

"Aaron?"

The dense fog around him was spinning, and Dustin faded in and out of view. He tried to run , but his legs had turned to lead and he could barely lift them. Confused, he saw the ground start to bend up and move towards him. He closed his eyes and cried out.

\* \* \*

Dan continued to watch from a distance as he'd agreed to do with Aaron. The fog was getting thicker and it was hard to see the pair clearly, but he'd heard everything, and was struggling to stop the tears from rolling down his face. He looked on silently as Aaron's gaunt figure, outlined in black against the whiteness of the fog and lantern light, appeared to get up, spin around, and topple to the ground. He was about to leave his hiding spot and move in, but reminded himself of the promise he'd made to Aaron earlier that day.

"Sir, whatever happens, don't let Dustin know you're there. Just go home and if I don't show up for school again, report it. Report whatever you saw."

Hidden by the fog, he watched as Dustin grabbed the lantern, scooped Aaron up into his arms, and walked off into the distance.

## Chapter Thirty-Three

Dustin approached the house and was relieved to
find the lights off and the driveway empty once
again. Magda was going to kill him anyway, but at
least he didn't have to face it until Aaron was safe.
He fumbled in Aaron's pockets for his keys, and
opened up the front door. It was almost like de-ja-
vu, but thankfully this time Aaron wasn't soaking
wet or fighting off hypothermia.

He still wasn't going to be able to get him up the
stairs like this, though. His plan had been to give
him the option of thinking that this was all a dream
by putting him into bed as he had done before, but
he needed to hoist him up like he had done last

time.

Dustin rested Aaron's limp body against the wall and checked to see that he was still breathing normally. He seemed fine, but whenever Dustin tried to wake him up he got nowhere. He hoped he was okay.

Pulling Aaron's arms over his shoulders, he lifted him up onto his back and slowly made the way up the stairs to his bedroom.

Kicking the door open, he rolled Aaron's limp body down onto the bed and flicked on the light. Not knowing how long Magda was going to be out for, he needed to be quick if he didn't want to get caught. He pulled off Aaron's top, his jeans, and his socks, leaving him in just his underwear, and pulled the duvet over him.

There, he thought, it's *just* possible that he'll believe it was all a dream.

Dustin walked over to the wardrobe and hung back up the clothes that Aaron had been wearing. Hopefully that'd throw him off the scent, too. He looked around the room as he folded up the socks and put them back onto the shelf that other socks seemed to be on, noticing a muddy looking journal on the desk by his door.

He moved over to it and looked at the page that was open, shocked to see his name appear.

'I am making progress with Dustin. I think he knows far more than he is letting on…'

What on earth? Who had been writing this, was it Aaron's journal? He flicked back through and saw two distinctly different styles of handwriting going right back to near the start. He read with interest and it suddenly dawned on him. He flicked to the front to see the initials carved into the now-mud-covered book. Xander's initials.

'It's not my feelings that matter, I need to solve this case! Why won't anyone believe me?' And then just below, in different handwriting, 'I'm Aaron. I think I believe you.'

Aaron had found Xander's journal, and started talking to him through it. Suddenly, it all made sense. Once Emma's personality had been lost, Xander's lingered. He'd comforted an upset Dustin, and this must all have spiralled from there.

Dustin heard the sound of pebbles crunching beneath a car tyre and, dropping the journal back to the desk, quickly moved over and turned of Aaron's bedroom light. Peering through the window, he could see a car pulling up into the driveway—

Magda was home.

Panicking, Dustin flew down the stairs. The headlights were bright through the small windows at the top of the front door, blocking the exit that Dustin was hoping to take. Speeding, he ran into the kitchen and flung open the back door. Thankfully the conservatory door lock on the inside was a turn-mechanism, and pulling the kitchen door closed behind him he flung himself out through the outer conservatory door and kicked the door closed just as he heard the front door slam at the front of the house. Running, his heart pounding, he headed for the clearing in the woods and the path back home.

## Chapter Thirty-Four

Magda closed the door behind her and called up the stairs.

"Aaron? Are you home?"

Moving into the living room, she dropped her bag down on the sofa and pulled out her notepad. She'd been at the council offices for what felt like hours, teaming up with other campaigners about the housing development on the land by the house, and needed to make sense of the copious scribbling she had made in her native German before typing up a report in English to post to the website.

"Aaron?"

She plodded up the stairs and opened Aaron's bedroom door. There, in his bed, Aaron was sleeping peacefully.

"Aaron, dear?"

No response. He was obviously exhausted and had decided to go straight to bed when he'd got home from school. She closed the door gently and headed back downstairs.

She stepped into the kitchen and switched on the light. His bike was there as usual, but the door between the kitchen and the conservatory was open. Checking the door, she realised it was unlocked.

"Verdammt noch mal, Aaron. Must have forgotten to lock the door when he came in. We'll have thieves all around when the new houses are built…"

She locked the door and, heading back into the kitchen, put on the kettle and started making her usual aperitif of ginger tea. With Aaron already in bed, she could focus on her notes for the rest of the evening. As the kettle boiled, she pulled out a piece of paper and grabbed the pen she kept on the side for note making.

'Hello Kleine' she wrote. 'Hope you caught up on sleep, you must have been really tired when you got home from school! You left the door unlocked, please try not to do that. See you tomorrow, don't forget your medicine!'

She put down the pen, poured the hot water into the waiting tea cup, and shuffled out of the kitchen and into the living room where she did the majority of her work. All of the campaigning against the recently approved housing development was taking up a lot of her time, and she felt a twinge of guilt that she hadn't done much to engage with Aaron in the evenings when he was home from school.

She worried, too, about how Aaron was doing. It wasn't normal for a teenage boy to come home from school and crash out in bed, was it? Maybe it was. She felt utterly lost and without guidance. It was her own fault, she supposed. She'd deliberately told the doctors that she was happy to go it alone.

The last thing she wanted was for her family to become a source of town gossip, so she always hid their troubles or woes from the world. Whether it was her husband passing away or Aaron's condition, she kept herself to herself and made lots of noise about the things that had nothing to do with her family.

She was a proud woman, and it was just her way of

getting by.

Magda pulled the notes from her bag and sat down at her computer. Typing these up would distract her, and she enjoyed feeling like she had a purpose. She liked that the people of the local activist committee looked up to her, and that the town council feared her.

Tapping away at her keyboard, she stopped and looked upwards. Hopefully this was all just temporary, she thought. Aaron's condition would stabilise and he'd be back to his old… well… his whole self again soon.

## Chapter Thirty-Five

Dan was cold.

Again.

Sitting in his classroom on his computer, he had hoped that at least a little heat from the machine in front of him would start to raise the temperature— but he was still sat in a scarf and his thick coat. As he was getting out his planner, he heard the sound of a knock on his classroom door.

"Come in, it's unlocked!"

The door opened and Aaron Grayling walked through it.

"De-ja-vu" said Dan, before moving to a more sensitive tone. "Are... are you okay? After last night I thought..."

"I know, I'm so sorry about that. I must have got home and fallen asleep. I woke up and it was like 4am, so I knew I'd missed my chance with Dustin. How long did you wait out there before giving up?"

"I, err, what?"

"You *did* go, didn't you? I know it was asking a huge favour but you *did* agree. Did Dustin actually show up?"

"I... err... yes. But what did you say happened to you?"

"I woke up in my bed at about 4am this morning. I must have laid down as I was getting changed and fallen asleep. I'm kicking myself. I had another weird dream too, though I can only remember bits and pieces."

"You, err, um. I mean, err."

"Sir, are you okay? You're stuttering more than usual, I thought we'd got past that?"

"What I meant was, err, what was your dream?"

"Well, I was with Dustin, but it was foggy and I

couldn't see much else. We were just sat there talking, two people in all this fog."

"Right. And, err, what were you talking about?"

"I said that Emma, that's the person who got killed, wasn't actually killed. I'm trying to remember it exactly, everything's a bit hazy."

"Was it that she was the…"

The two then spoke in unison:

"…same person as X?"

"How did you know that?" Demanded Aaron. "How could you possibly know what Dustin had said in my…"

"Aaron, I was there. It, err, it was real."

"It was real? Wait, it wasn't a dream?"

"No, All that stuff Dustin said, he really said it, and you passed out and I, err, I think he took you home."

"It's coming back to me, but it's still not all there. Why did I pass out? Did he try to kill me?"

"No, I think it was, err, umm, kind of, well, I guess it was the…"

"The what, Mr. Varley?"

"Well. I don't want to lie to you. I think it was the weight of hearing that you were in fact the killer that you'd been looking for."

Suddenly it was as if the curtain covering the truth had been yanked back., and Aaron could remember the events of the night before with a sudden clarity. He was the window. He was the one with the disorder.

"I… I'm… I have…"

"DID, yes. Although I think the way that Dustin put it was very poetic, and really made me think about it in a new light. I mean, before I'd sort of seen it as a disorder, something to be afraid of, but when he-"

"You knew? All this time you knew and I didn't?" Aaron sounded angry.

"I, err, well. I didn't know everything. I'd just heard rumours, in the staff room and around school. Only the head actually knows your actual medical situation."

"Is that why you were avoiding me?"

"I, err… yes. I'm sorry. I didn't understand it."

"Nor do I. Why do I have no memory of this? If

I'm the one that chose to take medication, why can't I remember doing it? Why have I just been blindly taking tablets every morning without questioning why? My Mum…. She must know, surely? She must be the one feeding me all these pills and lies. She… I mean… Grrrrr!"

Aaron looked distressed, and his anger pulsed out of him as he hit a nearby desk. Dan had no idea what to do, no idea how he must be feeling. He couldn't empathise, and he could barely comprehend it. All he knew is that, after hearing Dustin last night, his understanding of the situation had been turned on its head. He felt a huge amount of sympathy for Aaron, like he might be the only real innocent victim in all of this.

"Aaron. I, err, look, I mean, you… I'm sorry."

Aaron stood in front of his tutor, fists clenched, face red, shaking. Dan noticed a glimmer appear in his eyes, and within a few seconds streams of tears had started falling down his face. His body shook and convulsed as all of the rage and anger within him turned into water in his tear ducts.

Dan had no idea what to do. Putting a hand on Aaron's shoulder and breaking every single rule of his profession, he reached up and gave Aaron an awkward hug. The height difference was staggering, and Dan fully expected Aaron to recoil away, but instead the teenager arched his back, threw his arms around him, and stood sobbing into his tutor's shoulder.

Minutes went past, and eventually Aaron broke away and collapsed into a chair. Dan, shoulder wet from Aaron's tears, moved over and sat in a chair opposite him.

"Do you want me to send a note round to your teachers saying you've got coursework to catch up on, and so are working from here for the day? I've got some classes, but you can sit in the corner on a computer and be safe and left alone?"

Aaron nodded. Dan had no idea what to do, but knew that a can of worms had been opened and there was no going back to pretending he didn't have a stake in the situation. He didn't know much, but instinct was telling him that Aaron couldn't face anyone right now, and he needed to be somewhere safe to rebuild some of his strength.

"Why don't you grab that machine in the corner then, over by my desk. I was about to go and make myself a cup of tea, actually, do you want one?"

Aaron nodded, clearly dumbfounded and distressed.

"Okay. Well hey, we'll get through this, okay? I, err, I actually really admire your strength."

Dan grabbed the mug from his desk and headed to the door.

"Sir?"

Aaron's cracked, tear-worn voice trembled across the empty room.

"Yes?"

"Thank you. For everything."

## Chapter Thirty-Six

In spite of having tried for hours, Dustin just couldn't get to sleep last night. Looking over at his phone he realised that it was 11am, and while it was his day off he really hated staying in bed this long.

"Come on Dustin" he said aloud. "Get out of bed."

He was grateful to not have to work today. Last night's encounter with Aaron had taken the wind out of his sails and he couldn't help but worry about how he was doing after having to put him to bed again. In a way, it reminded him of some of the evenings out he'd have with Emma, sneaking home at all hours after a night of cuddling and listening to music in the woods.

God, he missed Emma.

He rolled over and faced the wall. He hadn't known what he was getting himself into, but he wouldn't take it back for the world. Not one second of it. He closed his eyes, and let his mind think back to happier days.

Out of nowhere, he heard his phone beep. Given last night's events, he had a feeling he knew who'd be messaging him at this time on a Tuesday. He reached behind him and grabbed his phone from under his pillow. Focusing his eyes on the notification, he was apprehensive. As he suspected, it was from Aaron.

'How did I get home last night?'

So, he remembered. Dustin's plan had failed, and Aaron wanted yet more answers. What was the point in hiding anything anymore?

'I carried you. You passed out. Are you okay? How much do you remember?'

'I remember it all now. Wasn't sure when I woke up but it's all come back to me now. I'm sat looking everything up online.'

There really was no going back now, was there? Dustin shook his head. What would this mean for Aaron, and what would it mean for him? Magda was likely to be angry.

'Don't believe everything you read. Where are you?'

'At school. Only place I felt safe this morning.'

Makes sense, he thought. School had always been a place that Aaron loved, it let his studious nature out. No matter who he was fronting as, a love of knowledge and learning always seemed to shine through. Another message from Aaron came through before he had a chance to reply:

'Thank you for the truth. And for getting me home.'

Dustin just stared at his phone blankly, not really sure what to think or feel or say. When he'd first met Emma, he'd adjusted to dating a trans girl quickly— it wasn't something he'd really put much thought into previously, but it felt natural to him and after the first couple of weeks he hadn't given it a second thought.

Finding out that Emma was Aaron, and Xander, and all the others… that had taken some adjustment. But he loved her intensely, and was prepared to stand by her no matter what. Magda had been supportive of their relationship at first, seeing the joy that it brought to her… or him… them… damn it, pronouns were hard when they kept changing.

Dustin had given up a lot to stay with Emma, including a place at university. And now, it barely seemed worth it. Still, seeing a text like that from Aaron felt warm. It felt happy and safe and good. As long as he was helping Aaron, at least, that was at least a positive in all of this.

'You're welcome, man' Dustin replied. 'What are you going to do?'

A reply came in fairly fast.

'She's been lying to me this whole time. I'm going to confront her. I've got to talk to my Mum.'

Dustin knew Magda, and knew that it wasn't going to be an easy discussion. Things weren't great in her life either, and she'd really struggled with Aaron while he was presenting more plurally.

'Are you sure? Do you want someone else to be there?'

Another fast reply.

'No, I have to face this on my own with her. She has

been lying to me all the time, forcing medication on me… not that I've been taking it… and she needs to give me answers. At least you eventually came clean and admitted to the deception. I have to know why, and I have to know how.'

'Stay safe, Aaron. I'm here if you need me.'

'I think you've done enough. I am so sorry about Emma.'

Seeing her name was always hard for Dustin, but seeing Aaron apologies for her no longer being with them really struck a chord. What was he sorry for?

'Don't be sorry.'

'Dustin, you deserved better. Thank you for everything.'

Thank you for everything? That sounded more like the kind of thing people said before disappearing. Maybe he was overreacting. He had a habit of doing that. Rolling over, he put his phone back under his pillow and closed his eyes.

"Good luck, my friend."

And with that, he finally drifted off to sleep.

Kestral Gaian

## Chapter Thirty-Seven

Aaron burst through the back door with his fists clenched, breathing heavily. His bike lay on the floor of the conservatory, abandoned with the same anger that he now exuded. The noise of the door slamming open roused Magda, who had been in the living room on her laptop, and after a few seconds she appeared in the kitchen doorway.

His anger burned hot and tears filled his eyes, stinging his face. This was it, he thought. The final confrontation. She couldn't hide anything from him now.

"Oh my goodness, Kleine, what happened? Are you

alri-"

"SHUT UP"

Aaron screamed at his mother. The shock of his words stunned her into silence, but it was like a gun had fired from his throat. He went to step forward, but lost his footing and fell to his knees. Suddenly the tears of anger turned to a waterfall, and he convulsed as it overcame him.

"How could you, Mama?" He sobbed.

Aaron felt his mother's arm around him, and he recoiled away.

"What's going on? What happened?"

"Dustin… Emma… I'm…"

"Oh. I see. I'm going to kill that boy."

"It's not his fault. How could you?"

"We're not going to talk about this. It's no-"

"Yes, we are."

Aaron got to his feet as his brain managed to find a way to pump some adrenaline through his veins. He felt powerful, in control.

"You are going to sit down, and we are going to talk

about this. Right. Now."

Magda pulled out a chair and sat down. Aaron couldn't quite make out her facial expression—it was half indignant, and half in shock. He really didn't talk to her like this. Hell, he didn't talk to *anyone* like this. But this was his life, his memories. She'd been lying to him and he had to confront her on it.

"I have spent the entire day online, Mama. Researching. Looking things up. Do you know what it's like to have to read that the medication you're on may result in memory loss in the first six months of use? To read stories of people in my exact situation whose parents and families have helped to remind them each day who they are and why it matters?"

"Aaron, I-"

"You've lied to me. That's what you've done. You had every chance to tell me who I am, to explain the whole situation to me and keep reminding me why I was taking the medication I was taking. I gave you chances to come clean about Emma and you lied to my face. I even saw you and Dustin talking, and you pretended not to know him when I asked about him later that same day! You lied. You thought that keeping it from me was a better option."

"I just tho-"

"No, Mama. This is *my* life. How *dare* you?"

"I…"

"Here's what you're going to do. You're going to explain everything, from the start. Because right now, the way I see it, is that you're nothing more than an accessory to murder. Emma, Xander, and all the others… you bought the gun and you kept supplying the bullets. So start talking, start at the beginning, and I don't want to hear a single damn excuse."

"Baby lamb, this whole time I've just been trying to protect you…"

Aaron could see that she was upset by his words, but it was too late. He needed these answers. There'd be time for healing later.

"Mama, please. From the start."

"Auch du lieber Himmel. Alright. You have… certain issues, Kleine. A few years ago you were diagnosed with"

"With an Identity Disorder?"

"Yes, DID. Multiple personalities. I mean, the signs were there early on and we knew something was different about you but it was only as you got older that it got clearer and the doctors were finally able to do something."

"Start at the *beginning*, Mum. Please."

"Your father doted on you. He was always very reluctant to admit there was something wrong with you. When you were das Kleinkind, you used to want to be called by different names and wear boy clothes one day, girl clothes another day. We talked it over and concluded you might be transgender and that we'd support you in that. Your father had always wanted a daughter and he loved the days that you were Emma more than the days that you weren't."

"I… he…"

"Please understand that we wanted to support you whatever your identity was. We thought you were going to want to transition to one thing or the other eventually, but as you got a little older the personalities became more… defined. More *gesondert*. You were one person and then another and then another. When your father died we didn't hear from Emma for a while, and a few new names popped up. It was like you had no idea who you were. It was scary."

"For who?"

"All of us, Kleine. I had lost my husband, and it felt like I was losing you, too. But it got worse as you hit Jugendweihe. It went from something almost playful to being something angry. It would switch more often. You'd go out roaming in the middle of the night. There were so many people inside you trying to get out that not a single one of them got enough time to live a full life. And then Emma met Dustin and that relationship started. It was all too much."

"*For Who?*" Aaron repeated, frustration clear in his voice.

"Aaron, *please*. You wanted to know the whole story. Just listen. We spent a lot of time in the hospital and with doctors working out what exactly was happening and how we could help you. No matter who we talked to, whether it was you or Emma or any of the others, all you wanted was stability. It was exhausting you, draining you completely. You were missing school. And none of the small-dose medicine that we were trying did anything."

"And Dustin…"

"Obviously Dustin wanted to see as much of Emma as he could. And I wanted to see you happy. When Emma was around Dustin she was always in such a fantastic mood, and he really did love her. He never cared what was between her legs. But it wasn't stable. Nothing was stable. And finally the doctors offered a solution to it all, medication that they hoped would suppress things and make you one whole normal person."

"*Normal?*"

"You know what I mean. Something that would stop you flashing from one person to another to another all the time. Calm you down and let you actually have a life. We argued a lot about it. Dustin argued too, with Emma. But eventually you, the real you—Aaron—you came to your senses and agreed. The doctors said it works differently on different people, and the side effects could last a few months. They recommended we be honest and open with you but I just wanted you to be a normal teenager. I wanted you to forget all of the pain and just be you. So when your memories got muddled and fuzzy I just… didn't correct you."

"How *dare* you?" Aaron's anger was rising to the surface again and he sat forward, spitting his words at his mother. "How dare you decide what I need to know. How can I *ever* trust you again?"

Magda's eyes filled with tears.

"I know, Kleine. I know. I took it too far. When you had questions, I'd lie. When you asked things that I thought might lead you to a discovery, I'd point you in another direction. I'd destroy evidence, I burned possessions… I just thought I was helping you get better. Dustin *promised* me he'd keep the secret. I Can't believe he told you. He just-"

"He only told me because I asked. You spent so long covering your tracks and remembering your lies that you forgot to check how I was really doing, Mama. I was having dreams, people were screaming at me, telling me that they were dying. I could barely sleep. I found a journal that Xander was writing."

"I thought I'd thrown out all of his journals."

"It was hidden in the woods. I guess now I know why. He was responding to me. And you're telling me that all this time, I was talking to… myself? And you could have told me, you could have set my mind at ease but you didn't."

"But how did Xander know about-"

"He didn't. But he knew Dustin. He worked out that someone called Emma had gone missing and he was investigating it. He'd even gone to the police about it. But when they refused to help him he started writing the journal that I then found in the woods."

"The police knew about your… situation. There had been a few run ins."

"So not one of you wanted to tell me the truth? Every single person in this town that was meant to protect me failed. And as a result, I've spent the best part of three months trying to solve a murder when the entire time I was both the killer and the victim?"

"Aaron, I am so sorry. I am just s-"

"And every morning you'd feed me tablets telling me that I needed them, but never telling me why. I took them because I trusted you. Is that why you never gave me the actual medicine bottle? Were you worried I'd look up the medication and realise what you were dosing me with?"

"It was your choice, dear. *You* chose to ta-"

"But I don't remember making that choice. Show me. Show me what I'm taking."

Aaron shook with rage as his mother, eyes still full of tears, reached down into the handbag she'd left on the table earlier that day. She pulled out a large,

pink tube full of tablets and handed them over to
Aaron.

"There. I just picked up the next three months
worth a few days ago."

Aaron looked down and the bottle in his hands,
turning it over and over as the pills rattled against
the plastic. He was overwhelmed with it all—the
betrayal from his mother, the guilt he felt for
murdering Emma, the shock at hearing the truth,
and the pain he now knew that his actions had
caused Dustin. It boiled up inside him like a sea of
acid trying to reach his eye sockets. Without
thinking, he flicked off the lid of the bottle.

"You know what, Mama? I'm done with this. I'm a
murderer, I've destroyed people's lives and dreams,
and I'm fundamentally broken. The people I trusted
most have betrayed me, and I've hurt the only ones
who loved me. You want me to be normal? Fine."

Putting the bottle to his lips, he turned it on its end
and  poured the entire contents into his mouth in
one go.

"NO! Aaron please, no!"

He swallowed hard, choking a little on the sheer size
of the mass he had just consumed. There was no

turning back now. It was done.

"Goodbye, Mama." He shouted, rage still flowing from him like a river of hatred and bile. "From all of us."

Turning his back on his now shaking mother, he pulled the back door open, pushed the conservatory door, and ran off into the dark and cold winter evening.

## Chapter Thirty-Eight

"Hello? Ambulance please. Thank you. Hello, yes, it's my son, he's just taken a lot of pills and has run off from the house. Yes it's Woodland House in Meriville. Yes. Aaron. Aaron Grayling. No they were pills he was already taking. They are chlorpromazine. Yes. He was just running, I tried to run after him but he was so fast. I think he went into the woods. Yes, the old station area. Okay. Please hurry. Yes, this number. Thank you."

Magda ended the call and looked down at her phone. How could she have been so stupid in giving Aaron the pill bottle knowing the state he was in? Would the ambulance arrive fast enough to get to him? She unlocked her phone again and scrolled to Dustin's contact card. Hesitating for a few seconds, she shook her head and hit call.

"Hello?"

"Dustin, it's Aaron. He overdosed on his medication and ran off into the woods."

"What?"

"After he found everything out, he came home and demanded answers. I explained everything and then he took the pills and took off running."

"I'll call an ambulance."

"I've already done that, but what if they don't get to him fast enough? You know those woods, all the places you used to hang out, will you go and look for him?"

"How many pills did he take?"

"A whole fresh bottle. I… I gave them to him."

There was silence, as the weight of the words settled in.

"I'll go and look for him."

And with that, the line went dead. Magda was left alone, shell shocked, staring at her phone.

\*　\*　\*

Aaron ran as fast as he could until his sides began to ache. He was deep into the woodland, far past the well-trodden path and somewhere in the area that the builders had closed off. Initially he was just running, but found himself drawn toward the old station that he'd been at with Dustin the night before. If only he could find it.

He was starting to feel sick, too. Dizziness was setting in, and he knew it was a direct result of the medication he'd just swallowed. He stopped to look around. Things were starting to get foggy. Was that the medication? Or perhaps… yes! He was near the lakes, which must mean he was getting close to the old ticket office buildings. Catching his breath he started moving again, staggering slightly but managing to put one foot in front of the other.

His stomach felt like it was on fire, and his body felt hot and clammy. He couldn't tell whether the latter was from the running or from the tablets, but he knew that something was happening. He felt drunk, and the world lurched and changed shape around him.

Finally he found a bench. A wall. Yes! This was the ticket office. The place where Dustin had told him everything. Where Emma and him used to… he couldn't remember. But he knew this place meant something. He tried to sit down on the bench, but by now he was shaking and far too dizzy to focus on what he was doing. He fell to the floor sobbing and, just before losing consciousness, he managed to squeeze out two last words:

"I'm sorry."

\* \* \*

"Aaron? Aaron!"

Dustin shouted as loud as he could as he hared through the dark woodland, the light from his torch bobbing in front of him. He'd been up and down the path that Aaron usually used to cycle along, and was now searching through the denser trees that led out to many of the haunts that he and Emma would spend time.

"Aaron? Are you there?"

He stopped to catch his breath, scanning around the area in front of him. This was useless, he thought. How was he going to be able to find Aaron in all of this? Was he too late already? Swallowing a whole bottle of pills... the consequences didn't bear thinking about. He'd already lost Emma, he wasn't about to lose Aaron too.

"I'm coming for you!"

Suddenly he had a thought, and changed tack. Darting past the felled tree and the old ditch, he made he way toward his familiar spot in amongst the ruins—the old ticket office.

The undergrowth was thick, and there were stings on his legs from the nettles that he was rushing through. It wasn't his usual route, but there was no time to change direction. He had to get there as fast as possible. Reaching the vague clearing, he called out once again.

"Aaron? Are you there Aaron?"

Moving towards the building, he noticed a figure on the floor. It was Aaron. He grabbed his phone and called the emergency services.

"Hello yes, Ambulance. Hi, yeah, you're already on

the way but I've found him, I've found Aaron Grayling. He's in the woods, by the old station. You can get close if you take the dirt path around the big lake. Okay, thanks."

He approached Aaron's body and, with relief, noticed that he was still breathing. It was shallow, though, and a quick hand on his forehead revealed the extreme height of his temperature. Dustin looked down at Aaron and welled up. Falling to his knees beside him, he wept.

"Oh, Aaron. Please. Don't go."

He put an arm under Aaron's shoulders and lifted him from the ground and into his arms. Embracing him, he heaved with tears of sadness and love as the blue lights of the ambulance approached behind them.

## Epilogue

Aaron awoke with a start. It was still dark, and a cool breeze washed over him from the open window next to his bed. He ran his hands through his hair— his forehead was clammy, and he noticed with annoyance that he had sweated through his bedsheets again.

Although… they weren't his bedsheets.

As his eyes adjusted, he could just about make out the room around him. This wasn't his bedroom—it looked more like a private hospital room. He tried to sit up, but he felt too weak. He noticed there was a lamp next to him, and fumbled around with his arm to find the switch.

Click.

He closed his eyes as light filled the room, waiting for them to adjust a little before he tried to open them again. Suddenly a familiar voice came from across the room.

"Aaron?"

"Dustin?"

As he spoke he heard how awful his voice sounded. Whatever he was doing here, he was clearly in need of medical attention.

"You're awake!"

"Barely… what happened?"

"You don't remember?"

"Everything's a bit.. give me a minute to wake up, okay?"

"Okay. I promised your Mum I'd text if you woke up overnight, so take your time."

As he lay there, eyes closed against the light that was penetrating his eyelids and making his vision a sort of pink mess of spirals and shapes, things started coming back to him.

He remembered the fog, the argument with his mother, his discussion with Dustin, and the hug he'd got from Dan Varley. Piece by piece, a picture of what had happened reformed in his mind. Only this time, it felt different. He felt somehow more complete, like something that had been missing was somehow part of him once again. He clenched his eyes closed against the light and tried to make sense of it.

"Are you okay? They pumped most of the bad stuff out of your stomach but they did say you weren't in the best shape. Do you want me to turn the light out again?"

"No. It's just… Dustin, I can feel them."

"You can what?"

"Like, I'm not them. But they're in here, somewhere. They're not dead, just… sleeping. But they're here."

Aaron felt something grab his hand, and flung his eyes open with a start. It was Dustin. He had tears in his eyes as he stood as his bedside, holding his hand. Aaron looked down and Dustin moved his hand away.

"Sorry, instinctive reaction…"

"No, it's… it's okay."

Dustin pulled a chair over to the side of the bed and took Aaron's hand into his again. They sat in silence for a while, Aaron staring up at the ceiling and Dustin moving his glance between Aaron, his phone, and their joined hands.

"I'll tell you one thing" Dustin said after what seemed like an hour of silence.

"What's that?" Croaked Aaron in reply.

"This would make one hell of a novel."

Aaron began to laugh, and he heard Dustin join him. Between sniggers, Aaron managed to get a few more raspy words out:

"You know what? You're probably right."

## Closing Remarks

Disassociative Identity Disorder, or Multiple
Personality Disorder as it used to be known, affects
around fifty million people worldwide. The story of
Aaron Grayling, whilst fictional, depicts a typical
scenario in which existing mental health conditions
are brought out to the fore during a traumatic life
event.

If you are affected by any of the issues in this book,
you can find resources and local helpline numbers
online at www.centreforglobalmentalhealth.org.

This book was written with help and support from many friends and acquaintances who have shared their mental health experiences with me in order for me to to shape the characters, their reactions, and their impact on each others lives in a way that respects their experiences and conditions. However, no two people are the same, and your experience with these topics may differ. My sincere thanks to those who helped educate me, who let me listen to their stories, and who helped to inspire a character I have come to love dearly.

Hidden Lives also touches briefly on transgender themes and explores gender identity in its many shapes and sizes. I would also like to thank the amazing network of friends and allies from within the trans community worldwide for their support, guidance, and continued friendship. I am truly lucky to know so many wonderful people.

If you'd like to learn more about gender identity and the resources available to trans people and trans youth, you can find more information and resources online at www.transyouthequality.org or www.wpath.org.

Made in the USA
Middletown, DE
22 May 2017